A Lady's Guide

to Passion and Property

A Lady's Guide to Passion and Property

Kate Moore

LYRICAL PRESS
Kensington Publishing Corp.
www.kensingtonbooks.com

In memory of my mother, Ruth Anne Kirby Hosken, 1923—2017, who set me on the path to writing heroine-centered novels set in England with her love of her father's native Dorset and her English aunties and cousins.

Acknowledgments

Jane Austen says, "We all have our best guides within us if only we would listen." It's writers like Miss Manners and Dear Sugar and Ella Berthoud and Susan Elderkin of *The Novel Cure* who remind us through their written guides of that clear wise voice within. It is in the spirit of those writers that I have written my guide for fictional heroines, and perhaps some living ones, as they search for the happiness of enduring love.

This second installment of the Husband Hunter's Guide series could not have been written without the support of family and friends. I began writing the book when my mom entered hospice and finished it after her passing. My husband, children, friends, colleagues, fellow writers of the Mill Valley Library Drop In group, my dearest brainstorming buddies, a nurse practitioner or two, and a pair of lively grandchildren have all provided needed cheer, wisdom, and help along the way.

In addition, Mom received kind and knowledgeable care from the Heartland Hospice team of San Rafael, and two extraordinary caregivers who came from England to be with Mom in the last months of her life. I hope Lucy, my heroine caregiver, reflects in part their patience and kindness.

I'm grateful for the patience and faith of my agent and editor.

Most readers of this slim volume are, no doubt, young women whose families have made some provision for them, however modest. Now we must consider two special cases from the ranks of husband hunters—the woman of property and the woman who possesses nothing but her shift. A woman who inherits a house, an income, or an estate may wrongly assume that she need not follow the practices outlined in this guide because she has suitors aplenty. Such thinking will be fatal to her happiness. Indeed, the woman of property must actively engage in husband hunting lest she mistake the ardor of her many suitors as desire to possess her rather than that most common of male desires—the desire to possess a pretty piece of property.

—The Husband Hunter's Guide to London

Chapter 1

The Tooth and Nail Inn

London, 1826

At the crunch of carriage wheels on gravel, Lucy Holbrook stuck a last branch of golden forsythia in a black jug on the sideboard of the Tooth and Nail's only private dining room. By placing the forsythia just so, she concealed a spot where the edge of the ivy wallpaper curled away from the wall. To Lucy the inn's flaws were as dear as its comforts, but she didn't want her home to appear shabby or rustic in her friends' eyes; and worse, she didn't want them to blame Papa for the inn's defects. She knew her father had meant to get to the wallpaper, and she was sure he had given her a childhood as golden as the flowers in the jug. She took a quick look around the dining room, prayed that its faults would be overlooked in the pleasure of the company, and descended to meet her guests.

The usual crowd of neighborhood men, who came for their daily pint and a smoke, had ceased their talk to gawk at the visitors on the landing as if the curtain had opened on a wonder at the St. Botolph's Fair sideshow.

The ladies, for their part, took no notice of the bench sitters. The twins, Cassandra and Cordelia Fawkener, in matching dark green, fur-lined cloaks, concentrated on removing blue kid gloves and black bonnets. The sisters were used to being remarked upon from their habit of dressing in matching outfits since their come-out some twenty years earlier.

Only Margaret Leach turned to Lucy with a broad smile and opened her arms. Lucy stepped without hesitation into her friend's embrace. A brief flood of memories washed over her. So many times at school when the subject of a girl's connections had arisen, Margaret had offered kindness and wisdom. Lucy had come to appreciate the distinctly feminine nature of such comfort. While he was alive, Papa had patted her shoulder and told her she would be a lady someday. And old Adam had mutely squeezed her hand when he sensed her distress. But her friend Margaret knew when to hold her. Enfolded in that familiar embrace against a silken, scented bosom, Lucy felt yet unshed tears threaten. She pulled back. Tears could wait.

"Dear Lucy," Cassandra began, turning her back on the public room, "we've been so worried."

Lucy smiled at that. "Surely not, though I expect you've been eager for me to return that third volume of Mrs. Raby's romance."

"To think of you here, alone, child," Cassandra added, draping her cloak on the growing stack in her footman's arms.

"Which you see I am not."

"Lucy"—Cordelia thrust a brown-paper-wrapped package at her— "we've brought you a gift. You must open it."

"Don't rush the girl, Cordelia," Cassandra advised.

Lucy thanked Cordelia and took the package. "I've a private room ready for our luncheon."

The ladies exchanged a glance of obvious relief and turned their backs on the bench sitters. As they climbed the stairs, Lucy took a moment to summon Hannah to help the footman with the cloaks and tell him that he might make himself at home in the taproom or the stables.

In the little room that she and Hannah and Ariel had done their best to smarten up, the ladies studied the cold collation Mrs. Vell, the inn cook, had consented to serve on a Sunday. Pigeon pie, sliced tongue, pickled eggs, and a glistening apricot pudding filled the inn's best plates, arranged on a clean white linen cloth with shining silver serving spoons. While the ladies filled their plates, Lucy poured glasses of a raspberry cordial she had persuaded Mrs. Vell to uncork.

"We have not put you to any trouble, I hope," Margaret said, looking up from the sideboard.

Lucy saw where Margaret's glance caught a yellowing water stain like a lace fringe above the bow window.

"None," Lucy insisted, unless one counted persuading Mrs. Vell to alter her time-honored patterns. "It's a cold collation, as our cook has strong feelings about Sunday cooking."

The ladies settled themselves at the table and gingerly picked at the food.

"We've missed you at services, dear. Our little readers' group is not complete without you," Margaret said. Their group called itself the Back Bench Lending Library from their habit of exchanging novels after services each week at the chapel in South Audley Street. Lucy had not joined them since her father's death a fortnight past.

"But we've brought you a book," Cordelia added, breaking off at a look from her sister. "Well, Cassandra, really, Lucy can see without unwrapping it that it is in fact a book, and what else, pray, would we be bringing?"

Most people could not tell the fashionable dark-haired twins apart until they spoke. Then Cassandra's forcefulness of personality made one notice the sharper arch of her brows and jut of her chin. And Cordelia's eagerness to please made one conscious of the softness about her mouth and eyes.

"Nevertheless, Cordelia," Cassandra said, turning to Lucy. "Before we get to the book, we must talk about your situation, dear girl."

"My *situation*?" Lucy held her fork suspended above a pickled egg. It was a careful word, a word that meant there was a problem to be dealt with, something that could be fixed or altered or improved, the way one cleaned a chimney that smoked or moved one's seat away from a draft.

The three ladies nodded in vigorous unity. Cassandra looked to the other two and clearly received some signal to proceed. "You do see that you must leave the inn."

Lucy put down her fork and slid her hand into her lap. She did not want her friends to see that hand tremble. She should not be surprised that they judged the inn as an unacceptable setting for a lady of their acquaintance.

"Yes, now that your dear father is gone," Cordelia added, "you may not stay in a common inn."

"But the inn is my home. It's where I live."

"It is what you've been accustomed to, to be sure," said Cordelia, "while your father was alive. However, a gentlewoman does not stay in a public house without a male relation on the premises and indeed without a female companion."

"Surely, my case is different, as I am now the innkeeper." Lucy watched Margaret for any sign that her dearest friend was on her side in the matter, but Margaret seemed intent on cutting a piece of tongue into the smallest possible bites. Margaret had been an instructor at Mrs. Thwayte's Seminary for Young Ladies in Hammersmith until she left to become the companion of the twins' elderly mother, Lady Eliza Fawkener. It was Margaret who had introduced Lucy to the twins and the Back Bench Lending Library group.

Cassandra pushed her untouched plate aside. "What you are, Lucy, is a woman of...property. You'll sell the inn of course," she announced.

"Sell the...inn?" Lucy had almost said *sell my home*, but she could see that her friends would be deaf to the claims of such a home with its noise and bustle, its rustic furnishings and humble hospitality.

"Once you've sold, you may convert the profits of the sale into the funds," Cassandra continued.

Lucy looked at the three solemn faces, alike in their expressions of certainty. Behind them the forsythia branch hid the wallpaper. They, too, had a plan for hiding any flaws Lucy might possess as she entered their world, such as being the daughter of a former pugilist who kept an inn.

At school, a girl named Amelia Fox had been the self-proclaimed expert on origins. "Your origins are your destiny," she would say, as she rated each girl's family ties. In Lucy's case Amelia had proclaimed that nothing could be done about her father, and it was just as well that nothing was known about Lucy's mother, because surely nothing good could be known. Now Lucy's friends invited her to shed her questionable birth forever with a simple economic transaction. As an heiress with her money in the funds, Lucy could slip into their world as if there'd never been a Papa, a Tom Holbrook, who'd once been Iron Tom in a bout against the champion. It was a tidy plan.

"Lucy, dear," Cordelia urged, "do open our gift. We found it in our pew, just where you usually sit, and knew at once that it was a sign." Cordelia gave the package a shove across the table toward Lucy.

"Not yet, Cordelia," Cassandra admonished. "Everyone should eat. I recommend this pudding. You may compliment your cook, Lucy."

* * * *

Captain Harry Clare, late of the First Royal Dragoons, opened the door of the Tooth and Nail, a west London inn from which coaches and travelers set out for Dover and the continent. He let in a gust of cold March air that caused the men on two long benches to glance his way and holler greetings. He had not encouraged the familiarity, but they greeted him as if he were one of their own.

He slipped out of his wet coat and hat and tossed them on a hook by the door. He had been lodging at the inn since the debacle that closed the Pantheon Club. The club, a front for a group of handpicked spies in

England's great game against her former ally, Russia, had been Harry's home for nearly a year as he and his fellow spies had tracked down enemy agents operating in London.

The club's unexpected closing had come just as Harry was about to complete his final assignment and receive the promised reward for his year and a day of service. Instead, he'd been cast out to shift for himself. He was an old hand at such shifts, having joined the army at seventeen and seen action from Spain to Waterloo. He could make a billet anywhere, from a muddy mountainside to the ruins of a shelled castle. And he was a man who never failed to complete an assignment, even one as puzzling as the one he'd been assigned—to find a blind man who was the only witness to a murder.

He'd found his unlikely murder witness at the Tooth and Nail, where the old man sat on a bench near the kitchen door, doing odd bits of handwork. The man, Adam Pickersgill, was simple-minded and easily agitated. A stray bit of conversation from the bench sitters could rouse Adam to a frenzy of waving fists and shouted words until his voice failed. Harry had seen similar cases of sudden starts in men who'd been subjected to the shock of war. Getting information out of Adam to solve a crime would not be easy.

The old man's daily pattern revolved around Lucy Holbrook, the innkeeper's daughter. She was a distracting female. The eye wanted to follow her, all golden hair and fair skin, but Harry was generally good at ignoring distractions when he had a job to do.

When he'd first come to the inn, he'd made an arrangement with the innkeeper, Tom Holbrook, about his lodging. In exchange for letting Tom set up a display cabinet at the front of the inn with the few mementos he'd acquired in the long campaign against Napoleon, he had a fine room. Tom Holbrook had fitted up a glass case in the entry to hold Harry's Waterloo relics: his straight sword, a bronze replica of the eagle he'd helped Alex Clark take from the French Guard, the *Morning Chronicle*'s report of his exploits, and a fine collection of Evershot plates depicting the heroes of June 18, 1815—Blücher, Wellington, and the Prince of Orange. If Harry thought the true heroes of the day lay in the fields of Belgium, he kept that thought to himself. He could tell a good war story with the best of them.

Then Tom Holbrook had been so inhospitable as to die. "Iron Tom," as he'd been known in his youthful days in the ring, had been buried the previous Sunday, and his golden-haired daughter had become a woman of property. The Tooth and Nail looked just as it had the week before, but its usual customers had taken to combing their hair and replacing stained waistcoats and worn jackets with Sunday finery. It was plain that, as the inn's new owner, Lucy Holbrook had become a sought-after prize. Harry was not a betting man, but he'd wager that the girl had other plans than marrying one of her neighbors.

From the entry, Harry stepped down the three wide steps that led to the common room. The inn's oak wainscoting was as brown as beef and ale. Its walls were gold as mustard or onions. Its hearths were black with a century's worth of soot.

Under the old mullioned windows facing the yard were the long tables where coach passengers could get a quick meal. A slate menu read: *Lamb. Pork. Beef.* A great stone inglenook fireplace divided the room between the front tables for travelers and the lowly benches in the tap where the inn's usual customers had their pints and smoked their pipes, dipping the stems in their ale.

The place was a bit of England for which the long war with France had been fought, but the men who sat on its benches knew war only as plunging or rising prices, changing governments, and distant battles that faded into history faster than the local champion's fame in the ring. They were civilians, and even after ten years of peace Harry didn't think he knew how to be one of them.

A thin layer of bluish smoke hung in the taproom air. The long-case clock ticked, the fire crackled, and outside, rain clattered in the drainpipes. The regular bench sitters slumped over their pint pots. Harry guessed the reason for their dejection—the innkeeper's golden-haired daughter was nowhere to be seen.

Will Wittering, a blacksmith with the forge that served the inn stables, called out, "Captain, come wet yer throat w' us this sad day."

Harry strolled their way, and the group shifted to make room for him on the bench.

"A bit of news for you, Captain," Will offered.

"What's that?" asked Harry. He nodded at Frank Blodget, the tapman, to draw him a pint. With the spy club closed, Harry no longer had to stick by its rule of no spirits.

"One of Sir Geoffrey Radcliffe's Rockets was stopped by a gang of highwaymen last night."

Harry took his first swallow of ale and listened as the tale poured out from several tellers. He took a moment to glance at the blind man, alone on his bench without his usual work. Queenie, the inn's orange-and-white cat, lay curled in Adam's lap between the big man's slack hands.

"Did the robbers get much?" he asked the bench sitters. He wondered whether he could get some sense out of the old fellow while Lucy Holbrook was away.

"That's the puzzle," said Will, shaking his head. "They only took the horses."

"Not Radcliffe's gold?" Harry knew the animals on one of Radcliffe's Rockets would hardly be prize horseflesh. Radcliffe ran the kind of coaching enterprise where profits were lean, and his drivers were the kind who drove their beasts until they died in the traces somewhere between London and Dover.

The bench sitters chuckled. Geoffrey Radcliffe had been knighted for loaning staggering sums to King George when the latter was a mere prince.

The bench sitters shook their heads. "A gang, they were," Will added. "Spoke some gibberish."

"Coulda been gypsies," suggested another bench sitter.

Harry ventured a glance at the blind man. It was a rare moment when Lucy Holbrook left the old man alone. Adam Pickersgill had been Harry's objective for weeks, but finding him had only deepened the mystery. Adam was tall and gaunt with a shock of white hair above a linen band that circled his head, covering his sightless eyes. Harry guessed his age to be near eighty and credited Lucy with keeping the old man clean and combed and neatly dressed.

Most days Adam sat on his bench with his brushes and blacking or a pile of silver and a pot of polish. The bench sitters knew little about him and cared less. Most of them simply considered the old man a fixture at the inn. He'd been there next to Lucy Holbrook as long as anyone remembered. Sheepishly, John Simkins, a merchant who sold water flasks, had confessed that as boys they had teased Adam and tried to provoke him whenever Lucy led him out of the inn for a bit of sun and air. How the girl had come to be responsible for the old man no one knew.

Harry turned back to the bench sitters, who were talking about roads and robberies and boasting that any one of them would have been a better match for the highwaymen than the coachman had been. It was pot-valiant talk, the kind Harry had heard from raw recruits on the night before battle. As the talk grew louder and bolder, the bench sitters glanced often at the door of the inn's private dining room. Harry suspected that at least three of them were working up the courage to solicit Lucy's hand in marriage.

"Where's Miss Holbrook?" he asked when talk of the robbery lapsed.

All the heads nodded at the door on the other side of the entry, and Will spoke for the group. "At luncheon with her lady friends."

Will wiped the foam from his lip. "Here's a puzzle for you, Captain," he said. "Why did Sir Geoffrey send his gold to Hell?"

Will, a fair-haired giant of man, was the wit of the group, and his companions waited for the punch line.

Harry shrugged.

"So he'll have some when he gets there," Will said. The bench sitters laughed and slapped their thighs.

"Geoffrey ran away." Adam Pickersgill's deep voice boomed out from his corner, stilling the laughter.

The men drew on their pipes. Harry nodded to them and turned to the old man.

"Geoffrey ran away," the old man repeated. His body shook the bench under him.

Harry crossed the room and put a steadying hand on the old man's shoulder, motioning Frank at the tap for a pint of small beer. When it arrived, Harry lifted the old man's big square hand and closed it around the pewter cup as he'd seen Lucy do.

Adam drank his beer in long drafts that left a foam moustache above his upper lip. He banged his cup down on the table, spilling ale. "Adam must not go. Adam must stay."

Queenie shifted her position in the old man's lap and jumped down to arch against Harry's booted calf. He leaned down to stroke the creature's head.

Adam stilled and cocked his head to the side. "You like cats very much."

"I do," Harry agreed.

The old man might be blind, but he was good at detecting a person's presence and recognizing people even before they spoke. If Harry could get Adam talking, he might eventually say something useful about the case. Harry suspected that Adam's odd declarations were part of a coherent story, fragments of a narrative in which one man ran away while another stood his ground, perhaps in the face of murder.

"Geoffrey ran away," Adam repeated, this time in the volume of ordinary conversation.

Harry gave Adam's shoulder a friendly squeeze. "How's the ale today, Adam?"

Adam's face crinkled into dozens of lines around the strip of unbleached linen. He reached out his hand for Harry's and gave it two long energetic pumps, like a man working a tap handle. "Tooth and Nail ale very good. You like yer ale very dark, like coffee."

"That I do, Adam."

From the benches came another mention of the robbery of Sir Geoffrey's Rocket passenger coach. Adam stirred, his gnarled hands pulling at the cloth over his knees. Harry sat down beside him, and Queenie leapt up into Harry's lap. He stroked the cat's fur and considered how to get the truth out of the old man's muddled brain.

* * * *

The scrape of spoons against dishes sounded loud in Lucy's ears, and she realized that the conversation had died and her friends were looking at her. She had no idea what they had been speaking of the past half hour.

"Lucy, child," Margaret broke the silence. "We really can't bear to think of you here alone, so far from friends."

Lucy held her tongue. *Alone?* She wanted to laugh at the notion. When was an innkeeper ever alone?

"A suitable place must be found to be sure, and we will help you." Cassandra spoke as if the matter had been decided over plates of pudding. "But you must quit the inn as soon as possible. Within a fortnight, at the latest."

"Sell within a fortnight? Is it possible?" She was not ready. Her future as a lady had seemed quite distant only a few weeks ago.

"Of course you will not handle the sale yourself," said Cassandra. "We will recommend a solicitor to make sure the inn's assets are properly valued. With the right help, you'll be ready to begin your London Season in days."

Her friends had worked out a solution to her situation. But a dead father was not a situation. The Tooth and Nail was not a situation. And Adam was not a situation. She did not know how she could begin to explain Adam to her friends, but there were things that could not be sold with tables and chairs, plate and silver, and stables and outbuildings. Even if one could sell everything one owned, one could not really sell one's past.

Margaret rose and came around the table to take Lucy by the hands, pull her from her chair, and fold her in another embrace. "Dear child, your future has arrived in a way none of us expected. Nevertheless, it has arrived, and your father himself, would want you to seek the best position for yourself in the world."

Lucy let herself be held. There was no denying that her father had wanted her to be a lady. When she was twelve, he had given her a painting of just the sort of lady she was meant to be. It hung in her room above the small hearth. Then he had sent her to Mrs. Thwayte's school, and when she had finished there, he had insisted that she spend Sundays with these very friends to grow accustomed to talk and manners quite different from those of the inn. Now, unexpectedly, the moment had arrived for her to step into the life for which he had prepared her. She simply had never imagined that she would step into that life without him.

Cordelia stood and once more offered Lucy the brown paper package. "Do open it, dear."

Lucy stepped back from Margaret's hold and tugged loose the string, unfolding the brown paper. A small blue book with gold lettering appeared— *The Husband Hunter's Guide to London.* She looked up into three bright smiles of encouragement. A hiccup of laughter escaped her. A month ago, two weeks ago, she would have devoured the little book eagerly, ready to learn its lessons. Now she understood that its lessons would be lessons in detaching herself from home. She wanted to toss the little book out the window and let the rain wash it away.

"You'll be brilliant, dear. We can't wait to help you enjoy a wonderful Season and a triumphant one," said Cassandra.

Lucy clasped the book hard lest she act on her first impulse. Her friends wanted the best for her even if they did not know what they asked in return—to detach herself from all that was known and loved. To adopt the ways she'd been learning in South Audley Street and to leave the ways of home behind.

A startling crash from the taproom interrupted her thoughts, followed by a man's anguished voice crying, "No, no, no, no, no."

The ladies started and looked confused. "What is that dreadful noise?" asked Cassandra.

The pained cry sounded again, louder still, full of terrible distress.

"Adam," Lucy cried. "I must go to him." She thrust the little book into Cordelia's hands and dashed for the door.

The woman of property may, for the most part, immediately dismiss from her court certain gentlemen who seek her out—the gazetted fortune hunter, the younger son, the widower with a needy family, the wastrel who has mortgaged his vast estate, and the handsome half-pay officer of the broad shoulders, gold epaulets, and frayed cuffs. These gentlemen have only one reason for marrying—the repair of their own damaged fortunes. Each of them has a grievance against the unfavorable circumstances that have cast him down. Self-interest both drives them and blinds them. Such a man will bend over the heiress's hand, thinking only of a new roof for the crumbling ancestral manor, a mother for the ungovernable children, or the grateful smiles of his tailor when his bill is paid. The woman of property must reject instantly any man who cannot see in her mind and spirit those qualities which will, when united with his own character, create a lifelong partnership.

—*The Husband Hunter's Guide to London*

Chapter 2

From the landing Lucy could see Adam standing in the middle of the room, his gnarled hands raised in fists. The bench sitters had scattered, clearing a space around the old man. There was only one man near him, the red-coated Captain Clare, the inn's most recent guest. His sharp warning glance checked her.

Adam stood like a tree on the heath in a gale, his body trembling. The painful memory that lived deep in his blasted, shaken frame roared like a caged beast. Lucy had been expecting an outburst since her father's death. Now it had come.

"Geoffrey ran away," Adam shouted, shaking his head. "Adam saw. Adam saw. Adam saw." He began to pound his head with his fists, crying, "No, no, no, no, no."

Lucy dashed down the stairs, but the captain stepped between her and Adam. She slammed hard against his red-jacketed chest, and he caught her by the shoulders. "He's not himself," he said in a low clipped voice. "He's been swinging those fists at anyone who comes near."

"Let me go. I can calm him." Lucy twisted in his hold and met his stern gaze with a steady one of her own. "I'm the only one who can."

The captain's grip tightened. His unyielding gaze measured hers. "Wait til he quiets."

"If he hears my voice, he will."

But Adam could not hear her. He repeated his pained cry. Behind her Lucy heard a gasp, from Cordelia she thought. She had not seen Adam so agitated in a long while.

His shouts rang loud in her ears until his voice grew raw and raspy, and his hands hung at his sides. The episode was over in a few minutes, but to Lucy it had seemed hours. The captain nodded and released her, and she crossed to Adam's side.

"It's Lucy, Adam. I'm here." She stood close enough that he could sense her presence. "I'm here."

After a long moment the old man spoke again. "Adam stay. Adam stay by Lucy," he said.

"Yes, Adam." She took one of the big fists and held it until the fingers relaxed, and she could take his hand. "You and I, Adam. We stay." She gave the old man's hand a tug, and he let her lead him back to his bench.

"Miss Holbrook." The captain's voice was low and calm. "Your guests."

Lucy looked up to see her friends on the landing wearing looks of shock and alarm. She had not realized how strange Adam would appear to them. A few yards separated Adam's bench from the little landing, scarcely enough room for five couples to move through the figures of a country dance, but it might as well be a gulf.

She glanced at the captain. "Adam needs me."

"I'll see the ladies out," he said. He turned away before she could thank him.

* * * *

Harry strode toward the three ladies standing with white, openly shocked faces on the landing. He'd seen them before, the twin sisters who dressed in matching gowns and their friend with the round face and brown curls peeping out from under a matronly lace cap, at the wedding of his friend Viscount Hazelwood. Lucy Holbrook had lofty friends for an innkeeper's daughter.

"Ladies, Captain Harry Clare at your service. May I escort you to your carriage?"

One of the twins, her hands clasping a little book to her breast, nodded earnestly, but the other drew herself up and demanded in a low voice intended for Harry alone, but quite audible in the silence, "Why isn't that man locked up?"

"I believe, ma'am," said Harry, glancing at Lucy leaning against Adam's shoulder, "that the old man lives here under the care of Miss Holbrook and her father."

"Her father is no longer with us. Some other place must be found for that man at once."

Harry bowed. "Shall I tell Miss Holbrook so by your request, ma'am?"

They could see Lucy's golden head against Adam's white one. It was hard to say who received more comfort from the contact.

The lady with the soft curls shook her head and quietly beckoned her friends into the private dining room. Harry followed them in and closed the door.

"Captain Clare," said the twin with the book, "are you a relation of Mountjoy?"

"His younger brother, ma'am." Harry could not prevent a tightening of his lips at the admission.

"Ah, we know your aunts." She seemed pleased to fit Harry into her world.

"Let me call your carriage, ma'am."

The bolder of the twins spoke up again. "You seem to be a man of sense, Captain. Reason with Miss Holbrook. She must not stay another night in such a place. We are prepared to take her with us this afternoon. Aren't we, ladies?"

Three faces turned to Harry full of concern and disapproval. They didn't like the inn, and they looked to be fixed in that opinion.

Harry did not think they would persuade the girl to leave the old man. What he saw in her was a dogged loyalty that no amount of condescension would dislodge. "I believe, ma'am, that Miss Holbrook regards herself as responsible for the old man."

"Absurd! A young woman, such as she, has no business being in charge of...a man. Can't one of those idle fellows be hired to mind him?" She gestured toward the common room.

Harry concealed a smile. The bench sitters might look idle, but they considered themselves the backbone of England, the men who did the work of the country. Even Frank Blodget, the inn's tapman, would regard the role of being Adam's minder as beneath his dignity. "I doubt it, ma'am."

"Please, excuse us, Captain," said the third lady, the woman of the soft brown curls and round face. "We are understandably concerned for our young friend. Is the old man any relation to Mr. Holbrook or his daughter?"

"None that I know of, ma'am."

"And has he no other recourse?"

"He's simple-minded, ma'am, and earns his keep doing handwork for the inn." It was not Harry's job to defend Adam Pickersgill from a world that had no use for the blind, but it was his job not to lose his witness.

"And does he often flare up in such an unmanageable way?"

"I couldn't say, ma'am. I've seen just the one episode."

"Thank you, Captain. Will you please summon our carriage?" She turned to the twins. "Let us make a plan."

"Ma'am." Harry nodded.

As he left the room, the first lady was saying, "We really cannot help Lucy if she remains *here*, Margaret."

He closed the door behind him. If Harry knew tactics at all, the ladies were regrouping for a further attack. They were determined to remove the girl from the inn. His aunts had descended on Mountjoy when his mother died, equally determined perhaps, but when they met his father and his brother, no silken sympathy and no effort to continue his mother's influence on that house had succeeded. Harry had joined the army within days.

Below him in the common room, the last bench sitter wiped the ale from his mouth, called a farewell to the tapman, and headed for the door. Harry followed the man out to summon the ladies' servants. When he had things in motion for their departure, he returned to the inn. Neither the girl nor the old man had moved. Harry approached cautiously until the girl sensed his presence. When she looked up, her eyes were deep pools of self-reproach.

"Your friends want you to leave the inn with them today."

She straightened at once. "They mean well, but I won't leave Adam."

"I'll sit with him while you say your farewells."

"You won't set him off again?"

"Talk from the benches set him off." Harry did not mention what that talk had been.

She whispered something to Adam and rose. Harry watched her cross the room with a light brisk step, momentarily distracted by the sway and rustle of her skirts. In minutes the ladies emerged from the private dining room, and the murmur of female voices—pleading and stern, and Lucy's quiet firm replies—reached the bench. Beside him Adam tensed, listening.

"I see Lucy, Adam," Harry reassured the old man. "She's saying farewell to her lady friends. She'll return soon." He kept his voice calm and matter-of-fact.

The footman appeared with the ladies' coats and cloaks, and when these were put on, Lucy steered her guests out through the inn door over their protests. Her friends might be interfering, but they offered escape. In Harry's experience it was the moment to run. He could see no advantage to the girl in staying to manage the Tooth and Nail, a form of drudgery in which she must soon grow old and coarse. He could imagine her friends urging her to take a husband. A husband, even one of her neighbors, would make a better partner than the old man.

In Lucy's absence Adam grew restless, his arms and legs twitching, until at last he leaned forward and laid his head and arms on the table. His mouth fell open, and he slept. Just when Harry thought her lofty friends must have snatched Lucy up in their carriage, she returned and stopped on the landing, looking lost and uncertain. When she caught his glance, she straightened and descended. He admired the effort to show no weakness.

"He's asleep." Harry stood and moved to cut her off before she reached the bench. He wanted to ask her about Adam without disturbing the man.

"What happened to him?" From his vantage point he could look down on the neat part at the top of her pale golden head. There was a simplicity to her dress and person that he preferred to the feathers and lace of her visitors. He wondered if she would lose that if her friends had their way.

"I used to ask Papa about Adam. I realize now that he told me very little. Only that Adam was in service in a great house before he came to us."

"A blind man in service?"

She shook her head. "I think he was attacked and blinded on the road and wandered to the inn. It was after the attack that my father cared for him." She shrugged. "And kept him with us."

The girl's explanation told him that she had little notion of the old man's past. Her father had told her a story that made sense of the old man's outbursts. But Harry guessed that the attack had been aimed at someone who mattered in England's wars, someone whose loss made the spymaster Goldsworthy put Harry on the case. The greater mystery was Tom Holbrook's part in the story. Why did a man with an inn and a family take on a burden like Adam? Most men would have offered alms and sent a stranger on his way. Harry was far from understanding why Tom Holbrook, by all accounts a practical man, had done something so unlikely.

"I have business to attend to this evening. Will you be able to manage him on your own?"

"As I have done most of my life?" She spoke defiantly, but she looked drawn, her eyes dark smudges in her pale face. "Pardon me. You've been helpful. Adam isn't very often so...agitated. It's only...that he doesn't like change."

"Sit down. You look burnt to cinders." His voice sounded harsh in his own ears. The thought of meeting with Richard had him on edge.

Her gray eyes flashed briefly. "Do you expect civilians to salute and obey, Captain?"

He smiled. He would like life outside the army better if he could give a few orders now and then and have them obeyed. "I expect a rational woman to behave with sense."

"Very well." She took a seat beside Adam, setting a little book on the bench beside her. The orange cat appeared and leapt into her lap, circled, and settled facedown against the girl's leg. Harry turned and strode away. He could count on the girl to keep the old man safe for the moment.

* * * *

Harry found his brother, Richard, Earl of Mountjoy, sunk in a chair in the subscription room of Richard's club, a glass of brandy in his hand. Harry supposed he should be shocked at Richard's appearance, the white hair and sallow skin tight on the bone, the watery eyes and thin frame. Richard had always been considered the handsomer of the two brothers. At forty-one he looked more like their father than the brother Harry had once followed on youthful adventures.

The hush of the club subscription room was nothing like the din of the Tooth and Nail. Every gentleman sat in an island of silence with his paper or his magazine. No one shouted for another round. Waiters came and went across the vast carpet, alert to a man's glance or his beckoning finger.

Richard looked up at Harry's approach, but did not stir, a man being careful not to jar his head. "Do you have it?"

"Hello, Dick."

"Don't 'hello' me, Harry. Do you have the blunt?"

"No."

Richard glared at him. "We had an agreement, Harry. Did you think I was jesting?"

"I didn't know you could jest." He had not heard his brother laugh in twelve years.

"I gave you a year to raise the money."

And Harry had been so close. One last assignment and he would have been paid for his year and a day of spy service to king and country. "Do you have another offer?"

Richard waved the brandy glass, sloshing its contents. "When I say the word, Finchley will get me all the offers I want."

Harry had no doubt it was true. Finchley, their dead father's man of business, must be eager to sell Mountjoy and see creditors paid and mortgages cleared.

"You're willing to let Mountjoy go, then?"

Richard snapped the fingers of his slack left hand. "Like that. Don't tell me that you are sentimental about soggy acres and that moldering ancestral pile you were so eager to leave?"

Harry looked away. No one in the subscription room seemed to note their conversation. "You know me better than that."

"Do I?" Richard started to shake his head, but winced at the movement. "I don't think I know you at all. Who are you? The bluff, hearty captain? The hero of Waterloo?"

"I'm a survivor, Dick. That's all."

Richard took a swallow of his brandy and wagged a finger at Harry. Apparently, he could still move his extremities, if not his head. "I know who you are. You're the spare who aspires to be the heir. You fancy being the next Earl of Mountjoy after I'm gone. You'll get yourself an heiress, sire some brats on her, and restore the noble line of the Clares. Duty and honor and all that rot, while me and my father will be a dead branch on the old family tree."

Harry did not answer. He had chosen years earlier to save himself. With an instinct for self-preservation, he had recognized his own danger, but he had apparently failed to see the danger to his older brother.

Richard stared into his glass. "I really shouldn't let you do it. The house is in shocking disorder. Tenants have fled. Rents are abysmal. Restoring the place is a pipe dream. Have you ever tried the pipe, Harry? Of course not. Father introduced me to it after you left."

"You could have stood up to him."

Richard brought his glass down on the arm of the chair, spilling more brandy. "Hah! You didn't stand up to him any more than I did. You ran away, remember."

It was an old accusation, and it should not sting, but Harry's jaw tightened. "I didn't follow him in every vice and folly."

Richard's eyes abruptly filled, and tears spilled over down the ruined cheeks. "Damn you, Harry. Remember, one offer is all I need, so if you're buying the Mountjoy mortgages, you'd better get your blunt together."

* * * *

When Harry returned hours later from his bitter meeting with Richard, he found the common room deserted, quieter than any camp the army ever made. He shook his head. He did not miss the bench sitters' boisterous camaraderie. He had regarded them as part of the furnishings, but now that they had vanished like the guests of an enchanted castle, he felt the life had gone out of the place.

Adam's bench, too, was nearly empty. The cat had taken Lucy's place, and the fire had sunk to a red glow in the grate. The girl's little book lay abandoned on the floor. He scooped it up, flipped it over, and read the title. *The Husband Hunter's Guide to London.* Perhaps it was a sign, the book that had helped Hazelwood crack their last case. Harry laughed at the idea, but another thought followed immediately. It was possible that he could use the book to his advantage. He dropped it in his pocket.

The cat lifted its head, arched its back, and mewed loudly for his attention.

As a woman of property is likely to receive several offers of marriage, it is necessary to consider the mode of a gentleman's declaration. There are gentlemen who, carried away by ardor or avarice, will rush to declare themselves without any regard for a woman's readiness to hear those addresses. There are other gentlemen of a more cunning and strategic disposition who will contrive the time and place, often public, of a declaration so as to ensure that a woman will have the utmost difficulty in refusing their proposals. And, there will be those men who from a spontaneous excess of feeling find themselves unable to offer a polished and coherent address, but only to press a woman's hand and gaze into her eyes. A woman may note these differences in the manner of a man's declaration, but of greater importance for her happiness is to note her suitor's words. She is advised to refuse any man who, in making his addresses, speaks principally of his happiness rather than hers.

—The Husband Hunter's Guide to London

Chapter 3

Lucy woke in Papa's chair, her feet curled under her, one of his old jackets over her. Adam snored peacefully in his bed. In sleep he looked untroubled, but she knew his past lay waiting for him.

Memory was a land Adam never traveled to except for those times when some word set off one of his frenzies. Then he became trapped in the past surrounded by things and people only he could see. The summer when she was twelve his spells had been alarmingly frequent. Lucy had written down all his odd pronouncements. She had taken the list to Papa to see whether together they might make a story of the disjointed fragments, but Papa had looked solemn and told her not to trouble herself to understand Adam, just to go on caring for him. He had taken the list from her and tucked it in the drawer where he kept Adam's things. Her gaze settled on that drawer at the bottom of the wardrobe. Now that she was solely responsible for Adam, she supposed that she should know more about him.

A knock on the door interrupted her thinking. Hannah called, and Lucy swung her feet to the floor. It was time to start her day. First, she would take care of Adam, then herself. Later, she would ask Captain Clare exactly what had disturbed Adam so deeply.

Once she had Adam settled on his bench, she dashed upstairs to her own room to put herself to rights for the day. She did not miss the book her friends had given her until she went to tie her ring of keys to the plain muslin pinny she wore over her mourning clothes. With her keys at her waist, she had looked up at the portrait over her small hearth.

The portrait, which was rather large for her room, had been a gift from her father when she started school. She had been reluctant to part from him, and he had presented her with the painting to remind her of the goal of becoming a lady. In the portrait, a true lady sat on a Turkey carpet spread on a vast lawn stretching up to a grand stone house. A little red book lay open against the lady's pale blue skirts. White lace at her sleeves and bodice caught the sunlight. The day must have been breezy, because the laughing lady held her hand to a straw bonnet with a fluttering blue ribbon that appeared ready to take flight.

Lucy had daydreamed of that picnic. But always she woke from those reveries to ask her lady questions. The lady only laughed and held onto her hat, so Lucy was none the wiser from her counsel. Lucy did not mean to be unjust to her lady, but she wished to know more of a lady's life than picnicking on the grass suggested. She wanted to know who baked the bread and packed the basket, who carried the blanket and heavy hamper out onto the lawn, what army of under-gardeners scythed the lawn, and who would wash the grass stains from the lady's white gown at the end of the day? She wanted to know how a lady mourned a father or bathed a frightened old man or stood up to the persuasion of friends.

As the familiar questions came, she missed the little book. Dimly she remembered putting it aside on Adam's bench. She had no use for *The Husband Hunter's Guide to London* now that Papa had died, but she would put it on her shelf and treasure it like the painting as a gift from those who loved her. Managing the inn and caring for Adam—those were her duties now and for the future.

By midmorning she and Hannah and Ariel had aired the sheets in three rooms, empty since the death of her father. She had conferred with Frank about the supplies of ale and spirits. And Mrs. Vell had informed her that no funds were available to purchase beef for the day's ordinary. She stopped on her way to the cashbox to look for her book under Adam's bench. It was his day to black boots. A row of scuffed footwear lined the bench beside him, while Queenie curled up in his basket of rags. There was no sign of the missing book under the bench or under Queenie. She stood trying to recall the moment it might have fallen, when she felt a tap on her shoulder. When she turned, she found herself face-to-face with Will Wittering in his Sunday best, or rather face to black-and-gold-striped waistcoat, for Will was a head taller than most men.

His thick golden hair curled over his ears. His beard was trimmed and combed. His ruddy face radiated confidence, and his large person blocked her view of the common room though she could hear the familiar murmur of male voices. "Miss Holbrook, a word," he said.

"Of course." She stopped where she was, conscious of his height and his size and a sense of some urgency compelling him.

Unexpectedly, he seized her hand in one of his own large ones and clung to it as a man washed overboard might cling to a line being dragged through rough seas. He squared his shoulders and took a deep breath like a bellows filling, and before she could stop him, a flow of words huffed out. "Miss Holbrook, the forge doing well this year puts me in a position to marry. I thought of you at once as just the woman for me, for yer not brought up too high and ye know the value of a pound. Ye could keep the inn, as I would keep the forge. And both would prosper. What do ye say?"

Lucy wished there were somewhere to look and some way to look that was less astonished and reluctant. Her lady would know what to do, but her lady was upstairs laughing and holding a bonnet to her head. Lucy's cheeks heated. She had the unpleasant sensation that everyone in the common room had heard Will's booming declaration. She pulled gently at her hand, and Will, as if just realizing the amount of pressure he had applied, released it. His open face lost a little of its sunny confidence.

"Mr. Wittering, I thank you for thinking of me as one who could contribute to your prosperity, but I must decline your offer at present. I must see what I can manage on my own before I join my enterprise with any other."

Will swallowed, his throat moving visibly, and plunged on as if she had not spoken. "I have three score horses on my books and what with hinge, bolt, and latch work, I might bring on a 'prentice this spring."

Lucy hardly knew what to say. He apparently chose to consider her refusal as a prompt for more financial information. "Thank you again, Will, but my answer remains no." She offered him a bow.

"Ye'll not find a better man in London, mind, so I'll ask again next quarter day, shall I?" He apparently took her astonished silence for agreement.

She gaped after him, and her gaze met Captain Clare's amused one. He raised his ale cup in a brief salute, his red coat unmistakable among the browns and grays of the bench sitters. He had seen and heard it all. Lucy escaped at once through the kitchen to the stillroom, where Hannah found her minutes later. Hannah bobbed a quick curtsy and announced, "A gentleman is waiting for ye in the council room. Stranded by a broken carriage wheel, 'e says. Says he knows yer da, but 'e didn't know yer da had a daughter. Did I do right to put 'im there?"

"You did, Hannah." She realized that Hannah looked to her for orders now.

"Oh, Miz 'olbrook, 'e's ever so fine with a gray coat. He says 'e's a sawbones, and 'e wishes to 'ave a supper. A bit of fish, 'e said." Hannah opened her palm, revealing a pair of coins that made a satisfying jingle. "Do we 'ave any fish for 'im?"

Lucy frowned. Mrs. Vell had not changed her menu in Lucy's lifetime.

Hannah jingled the coins in her hand again. "It's got to be the ordinary, don't it?"

Lucy shook her head. She was in charge now. She would run the inn her way. "If a gentleman desires fish, he shall have fish."

Hannah's brown eyes widened, and she closed her fist around the coins.

* * * *

Early in the afternoon, Harry went round to the defunct Pantheon Club. Outwardly, nothing had changed. The previous day's rain dripped from the scaffolding that concealed the building's stone façade. Loose canvas flapped fitfully in the wind. Harry tried the hidden door but found it locked. He strongly suspected that the elusive Samuel Goldsworthy, the spymaster who had recruited them all, was holed up inside.

Goldsworthy had pulled each of them—Blackstone, Hazelwood, and Harry—out of disaster with the promise of debts to be paid for a year and a day of service. Blackstone and Hazelwood had won their rewards, and Harry meant to have his. He gave the locked door a sharp rattle, but it remained closed. He stood for a moment listening to the drip of the rain. So far Richard's indolence and his disdain for money matters had served Harry well, but even his brother could not hold off creditors forever. Sooner rather than later, Richard would let Mountjoy Manor slip through his slack fingers. The club might be closed, but Harry still needed to buy up Richard's mortgages before someone else did.

The other entrance to the club was through Kirby & Son's Chemist shop around the block on Bond Street. Harry went round to the little shop. The bell jingled as he entered, and Kirby, the spies' tailor, looked up from behind the counter where he was assisting a gentleman with a purchase. Harry halted. He was used to seeing Kirby's daughter Miranda where her father now stood. It was one more sign of the closing of the club. He frowned and turned toward the shelves with their jars and tins and paper-wrapped soaps. The place smelled of lavender and citrus, like a field under the Spanish sun. While the customer dithered over his choice, Harry formed the jars and tins into a square on the shelf.

To Harry's mind the customer took an unconscionably long time deciding between one shaving soap and another. When the fellow finally left with his purchase, Harry greeted Kirby. "Where's the big man?" he asked.

"I couldn't say, Captain."

"Has Goldsworthy said anything about starting the club up again?"

"Not a thing."

Harry wanted to push on through the red velvet curtain at the rear of the shop, stride across the garden, and slip into the club as he'd done for the past year.

At that moment Miranda, Kirby's seventeen-year-old daughter and chief seamstress, burst through the curtain. Her gaze flew to Harry, and she checked her steps. "Oh, it's you."

"You were expecting someone else?"

She shrugged. "No one comes here anymore."

"Except customers, I imagine." He suspected she meant that no beaux came for her anymore, as the club's majordomo and junior spy, Nate Wilde, had done. The lad had been unable to resist Miranda's lush chestnut beauty from the first time he'd seen her. "Where's Wilde?" he asked.

Miranda tossed her curls. "I'm sure I don't know. You should look among his fine friends."

Harry nodded and went on arranging the jars on the shelf. She meant the Jones brothers, a trio of one-time bastards who'd risen in the world by taking on the powerful Duke of Wenlocke to save their youngest brother. The middle brother, Will Jones, had plucked Nate Wilde from a life of thievery in the darkest streets of London and made him into a first-rate aide on their cases. Harry didn't usually work with a partner, though Wilde might be useful. Wilde had a knack for disappearing in a crowd like one more London workingman.

"Thanks, Miranda. Shall I find Wilde and send him your way?"

She came around the counter and started to rearrange the jars and tins he'd displaced. "Of course not. I'm sure I've no thought of him in my head."

Harry grinned at her. The girl was a terrible liar.

She handed him a jar of scent. "Here's what you're looking for," she said.

He raised an eyebrow.

"I can take care of the captain's purchase, Father, if you want to have your tea."

Her father nodded and disappeared through the curtain. They could hear him shuffling along the hallway to the rear of the shop.

"Captain, I saw Mr. Goldsworthy go into the club this morning. Wait til Papa's at his tea, and I'll get you into the club," she whispered, and added in a louder voice, "And that'll be six and four."

"Thank you, Miranda." Harry stepped out of the little shop to wait.

The girl was as good as her word. Minutes later she led Harry through the shop and across the sodden garden to the rear of the club, using her own key to let him in.

She put a hand on his sleeve as he went to slip past her. "Can you get Mr. Goldsworthy to open the club again?"

"I mean to try," he said.

Inside the club cold and darkness reigned. Though they had been few in number, their band of spies had kept a kitchen and a small staff active. And always there had been the sound of hammers and saws as the work of perpetual renovation, part of the club's disguise, went on. Harry groped his way along the dark passage from the kitchen to the servants' stair and up to the first-floor coffee room. Velvet curtains drawn over the tall windows reduced the room to a shadowy cavern. Harry turned away from the empty couches and the cold ashy hearth. His glance caught on the leather gloves he and Blackstone had worn to spar with each other just days before the end. Blast Goldsworthy and the whole lot of them in the Foreign Office!

He took the wide center stairs up to the big man's office and opened the door.

By appearance and temperament Goldsworthy belonged more to the Tooth and Nail than to any gentlemen's club in London. Tall, bluff, and hearty, like a stout country farmer or a rich London merchant, Goldsworthy had a presence that filled a room. Behind his vast desk, he appeared as rough-surfaced and immovable as an ancient oak. The desk itself was more intimidating than a hillside gun battery with a sixteen-pounder trained on all who approached.

"Lad," Goldsworthy said, looking up, his big hands lying slack across the paper-strewn desk. "What brings you back? You can see we're quite closed down." A single lamp burned.

Harry stepped into the room. It was colder than the servants' stair. "Not me, sir. I'm still on assignment. When will the club reopen?"

Goldsworthy shook his great head with its russet locks. "These things take time. Government, you know, moves slowly."

Harry did know. He knew how often the army in Portugal or Spain had been left waiting for needed supplies promised to Wellington—men or horses, weapons, or even pay. It was a wonder that Wellington had won as many battles as he had. "What can we do to move the government along? Do we need to talk with Chartwell?" Lord Chartwell was the Foreign Office official with whom the spies dealt most directly.

"What we need, lad, is a big success."

"Shutting down a Russian agent and sending his British accomplice fleeing was not big enough for Chartwell?" Harry thought the spies had done quite well in their last adventure.

Goldsworthy's face didn't change, but Harry detected an uncharacteristic slump in the big man's shoulders. "It's true enough, lad, that we got Malikov, but Chartwell's convinced there's someone still out there, papers still going missing."

"And you sent me after a blind man?" Harry felt duped. He'd been hungry for action, and he'd been sent on a fool's errand.

"Did you find him?" Goldsworthy sat taller in his chair, an arrested look on his face.

"If I did, what would be the point?"

"All threads weave together, lad." Goldsworthy pinned him with a sharp gaze and repeated his question. "Did you find him?"

"I did."

"Good work, lad. You've not told a soul now, have you?"

"No one." From the big man's satisfaction, Harry could almost believe the blind man mattered. But Goldsworthy had not seen Adam Pickersgill shouting nonsense and waving his arms.

The big man nodded. "Has he talked?"

"He's simple-minded, sir. Childlike. He talks about cats and ale and his own daily tasks."

"You haven't asked him about the murder, then?" Goldsworthy started shuffling the papers on his desk. Goldsworthy's paper search tactic was one of the ways the big man kept his spies on their toes and in the dark. The man never parted with information easily.

Harry waited. For once he could bargain for information. He held a card the big man needed. "It would help to know who the victim was."

The paper shuffling stopped. Goldsworthy's face wore an expression of a man in the grip of the past. "One of our own."

"A member of the club? When?" Harry knew as he asked the question that it could not be a recent murder. For old blind Adam to have witnessed the murder, it must have happened years earlier.

Goldsworthy appeared lost in his own recollections. "Never mind, can the blind man talk?"

"I doubt he can tell us directly what he knows, but he has these fits or episodes when he says quite a bit, shouts wildly, as if some scene is being enacted in front of him."

"You've seen these episodes?"

Harry nodded. "One of them."

"Is the man mad?"

"More like he's caught up in the past."

"Where did you see the man's fit?"

"He occupies a bench in the public room at an inn." Harry watched the big man's countenance for any sign of recognition.

"An inn at the start of the Dover road?" Goldsworthy heaved his bulk up from the desk and crossed the room to a large map of London on the wall. He lit a second lamp and with a finger pointed to the inn's location. "The Tooth and Nail, is it?"

Harry nodded. "Some neighborhood men were talking about a stage coach robbery when something they said set the old man off."

Goldsworthy frowned. "So these episodes are seen and known in the neighborhood?"

"Common knowledge, sir."

Goldsworthy looked grave. His eyes shifted back and forth rapidly, a sign that he wanted action. "I don't like it," he said. "We have to keep the man safe until we can understand what he's saying. Take Wilde with you."

"So, you'll reopen the operation?"

Goldsworthy shook his head. "Never closed it, lad, but not a word to anyone."

"And the money?"

"All in good time." Goldsworthy waved a huge hand. "What do we know about the man? Anything?"

"His name is Adam Pickersgill. He was in service in a country house before he was blinded."

"Was blinded you say? Not born blind?"

Harry shook his head. The case meant something to Goldsworthy. The big man didn't want to let it go, even if his superiors at the Foreign Office came down hard. Harry offered another detail. "That's what the innkeeper's daughter says. According to her, Adam was blinded in an attack on the road and wandered into the Tooth and Nail, where her father took him in. Who was the target of that attack, sir? Surely, it was not a simple-minded servant."

Goldsworthy had a faraway look in his eyes. "One of our own, lad, one of our best agents."

"In what year?"

"It was '06. There were French agents in the émigré community acting against us. Our...man was about to expose an extremely dangerous enemy."

Goldsworthy shook himself, and the faraway look disappeared.

"I could keep Pickersgill safe until we're up and going again, sir, with a bit of blunt."

Goldsworthy's brows lifted, but he lumbered over to a cabinet piled high with rolled-up maps. With his broad back to Harry he opened the cabinet. Harry listened to the sound of a key turning, a metal lid opening, and the crackle of crisp paper. When Goldsworthy turned back, he offered Harry a sheaf of bank notes. "You'll report to me here. Make sure no one sees you coming or going."

It was a small victory. Harry kept his smile to himself and tucked the money in his pocket.

* * * *

With the spy club closed, Nate Wilde had found a room in the home of his friend and mentor Will Jones. For two weeks bells had rung in the grand house, but not for him. Every morning a tweenie laid his fire and a manservant brushed his coat. The butler said, "Very good, Mr. Wilde," as he came and went. It was everything he wanted, but not the way he wanted it. He hardly knew himself in his borrowed dignities.

Each morning of the first week he'd read the papers over coffee he didn't have to make and plates of eggs and bread he didn't have to clear away. The papers were full of apprenticeships and bankruptcies and situations for clerks, but a desk was the death of a man. If a man sat behind a desk, the world went by beyond his reach. His hands grew soft and white, his shoulders hunched, his waistline grew, and his ambitions shrank. A desk was no way for a man to make his mark in the world.

In the second week, Nate tried going with Will to the meetings of the parliamentary committee drafting Peel's act to make a London police force, but sitting in a room, listening to old men in wigs and whiskers argue about the difference between this word and that made him squirm. If he were a Member of Parliament, he'd drag the lot of them down to Bread Street to learn words they'd never heard before like *clicks* and *dibs* and *lagging* and what happened to a merchant's goods when someone cried *fat's a running*.

Today he'd left the parliamentary committee behind and headed out to confront London itself. Somewhere in the great sprawling city, a door would open for him. And when it did, he'd walk right in, and when he'd made his mark, he'd... But there was no use getting ahead of himself. Hours later his wanderings had led him nowhere but back to Bread Street where he'd been born.

The street had changed in seven years. Some of the old houses had been knocked down in the cleanup after the holding vats burst on the roof of Truman's Brewery at the top of the street. The beer flood had killed six people and splintered plaster-and-lath buildings on the east side of the street.

Then Sir Xander Jones had come with his East London Gas Company and torn up the streets and laid the pipes and put up lamps. They glowed now in the gloom of a dark wet day. Maybe it was those lights, but Nate thought more of the buildings had doors than he remembered, and in some windows he saw the answering glow of real candles. In one window at Number Forty, curtains hung. Bread Street was putting on airs.

It still stank of beer and piss, fish and turned oil. At the foot of the street he turned up the black velvet collar of an old coat he'd picked up from Bowen, a used clothes dealer on Monmouth Street. The green coat, stained and frayed at the edges, with one remaining button, covered his finery sufficiently that he thought he could walk the length of the street without any of its residents deciding to take a cosh to his head and empty his pockets.

His pockets were empty, as a precaution. He'd worn his oldest boots. New boots would invite trouble. His gaze swept the street for idlers at the usual corners where a cosh man might lie in wait. Just before the open court where the street took a bend to the west, a woman sat hunched on a step under a ragged shawl with a babe in her lap and a pint pot between her hands. A word would pass from her to her man around the corner as Nate passed. The iron cosh would slide down the man's sleeve into his hand, and the blow would descend before the woman stopped speaking.

Nate was an old hand at such lays. He could do the ambling shuffle that marked a man as a Bread Streeter, and snarl a greeting at the woman as savage as a punch. She lifted the pint pot and gave him a furtive glance.

Nate started walking, heading for the top of the street, where he could see the new vats at the brewery and the red brick corner of the school that had once belonged to Reverend Bredsell. He fingered the coins in his hand. He might get a bloater from the fish shop on the other side of the court for old times' sake.

The woman with the babe in her lap took instant note of his movement. She set her pint pot down upon the curb with a clink.

"Watcher lookin' fer, loovey?" she asked.

"A bloater'll do me."

"Yer a fine one, ain'tcha? Give a mite for the babe?" She extended a dirty open palm.

Nate ignored the woman's hand, watching the corner beyond her. As he came abreast of her, he heard the shuffle of feet scurrying his way.

He tossed a coin in the air, setting it spinning toward the woman, and lunged forward. As a man rushed out of the shadows, cosh raised, Nate dropped to a crouch, one leg extended behind him. He swung his back leg at the charging man's feet.

His attacker fell heavily, and Nate was up and on him, flipping the man onto his back and pounding the man's cosh hand against the paving stones until the iron bar clattered against the stones, and Nate snatched it up and thrust it in his pocket.

He stared down into a thin white face pitted with pox scars in which a pale beard struggled to grow and the eyes bulged. The man's chest heaved. He spat at Nate, and cried to the woman, "Do 'im, Biddy, ye useless female."

Biddy picked up her pint pot, sloshing its contents, and held it away from her. "It's a full pint, Tom. Ye never let me waste a pint."

"Do 'im, or ye'll feel my fist," Tom snarled.

Biddy lifted the pint pot, only slightly hampered by the babe. Nate held up a coin to show her. "I'll take that beer off ye, Biddy," he told her. "Put it down easy."

Biddy's gaze shifted from Tom to Nate's coin. The coin won. She lowered the pint pot to the cobbles. Nate tossed the coin into the middle of the street. Biddy scrambled after it and kept on scrambling into the court.

"Now, Tom," said Nate. "Yer drink's waiting for ye when we're done."

"I know you," the fallen man said. "Yer that bleedin' boy that brought down Bredsell."

Nate grinned. Now he knew why he'd come to Bread Street. He'd needed a fight, needed a foe, but a tougher one than Tom had proved to be.

In the old days Nate had been one of Bredsell's boys. He'd lived at the school and followed gentlemen and reported to Bredsell on their doings and been paid for it. And if he'd chanced to land before the Bow Street magistrate, Bredsell had arranged his release. At the time, Nate's great ambition had been to return to Bread Street one day as a High Mobsman with a purple silk waistcoat, rings on his fingers, and a gold watch as big as a turnip. He could laugh at those ambitions now. He had an account in Hammersley's Bank and shares in the East London Gas Company and more besides.

The fight he needed was not against the likes of Tom, but against a real foe, England's foe in the great game she played with Russia. Nate would go back to the club and rattle Goldsworthy's cage and get the old man to put him back on a case. Nate thought Captain Clare still had a case, and that would do for him.

As the husband hunter begins in earnest to seek her happiness, she assumes a new position of authority in her life. From childhood she has been guided in her choices by the wisdom of parents and guardians. But only she can be mistress of her heart. No one else can command its affections or inclinations. The husband she seeks will be that man who admires and respects her for her independence of spirit and habit of self-command.

—The Husband Hunter's Guide to London

Chapter 4

As long as Lucy could remember, Mrs. Winifred Vell ruled the Tooth and Nail's kitchen. She was a stout woman with a voice like a bagpipe and an appreciation for all things brown. She had two dutiful assistants in her twin children, Samson and Delilah, and was a great admirer of Vicar Rudd's stern wife.

Today Mrs. Vell wore a checked gown under her pinny as brown and white as her menu. A roast shoulder of mutton invariably followed a round of beef. Her whole desire for color was satisfied by the bright threads of the biblical scenes she embroidered for the altar cushions of the church. If culinary imagination was not her strong point, she did produce a great deal of food with clockwork predictability. Every morning a breakfast for the passengers arriving on the Rocket's night run, and later a dinner for the passengers on the afternoon stage.

She looked up with a frown at Lucy's request for fish for the gentleman guest. "Fish can't be had today. Too dear. And can't get a proper supper on for the stage folk by time and satisfy some gentleman's nice taste."

"Well then. I'll manage myself," said Lucy.

"Beggin' yer pardon, Miz 'olbrook, but this be my kitchen. Seven years I've put supper on for the stage passengers. Never missed. Never got it to 'em late. Yer papa and I, we had a bargain. 'Hear the horn; serve the corn.'"

"Just so, Mrs. Vell. Carry on. A plate for one guest need not interrupt the regular flow of beef from the inn kitchen to the table."

"Ye don't fool me, miss. Ye've no respect for the old ways. Yer papa not two weeks gone and ye be talkin' with gentlemen that be walkin' ruin in a red coat and wantin' to change things that ought not to be changed. If ye've no respect for gravy and biscuit and beef, then ye've no respect for Winifred Vell." She dusted the flour off her hands, shed her apron, and gathered up a straw bonnet, short brown cape, and her bag of needlework.

The usual fare for the stage passengers was headed for the door. Samson and Delilah left their posts and followed their mother.

"Not you, too?" Lucy had a foolish impulse to block their way.

"Where Mum goes, we go." Delilah bobbed a curtsy and followed Mrs. Vell. Samson shrugged and brought up the rear of the little procession of deserters. They marched out of the kitchen, Lucy trailing behind, past Adam's bench and the tap and into the common room. Lucy tried to think how to avoid a disaster.

Mrs. Vell sniffed and stopped to tie an elaborate russet bonnet over her cap. "Driven from my own kitchen, I am."

Lucy resisted an impulse to laugh. "Really, Mrs. Vell, I'm merely asking that you serve one guest a bit of fish. But if you cannot stray from the righteous path of beef, then thank you for your past service to the inn. You may expect a reckoning in the morning."

Mrs. Vell's cheeks shook, and she pointed a finger at Lucy. "Beware, miss. This is a respectable house. A girl in yer place to be wearing silks and talking with gentlemen in the private room—it be unseemly." She looked around. "And Pharaoh's lean kine et up seven years o' plenty." She strode toward the inn door, Samson and Delilah marching along behind her.

Lucy refused to glance at the bench sitters, witnesses to the little drama. Mrs. Vell's leaving would be the talk of the high street before supper. She crossed the room to the slate and wiped out *Beef Pork Lamb* with the palm of her hand and turned back to the kitchen.

By the fire, Adam sat polishing a boot, the cat curled against his thigh.

"Thank you, Adam."

"Geoffrey ran away." He repeated the sentence that so agitated him the day before.

Lucy put a hand on his shoulder. "No, Adam, only Mrs. Vell and her children."

"Adam must stay," he said, nodding his white head.

Lucy passed on to the kitchen. Without Mrs. Vell and her assistants, the room looked empty and vast, but there was soup simmering and fresh bread cooling. She rolled up her sleeves, wrapped her apron around her, and took a quick inventory of the larder. Her gentleman guest first. Stage passengers next. As long as she had Hannah and Ariel, they would manage.

* * * *

In the end Lucy decided that fish must do for both the afternoon stage passengers and the gentleman guest. The inn's benches were filled when she emerged from the kitchen at the sound of the stage arriving. No doubt news of Winifred Vell's leaving her post had spread up and down St. Botolph's high street, and anyone who could leave his business to run itself for half an hour had come to see how Miss Holbrook would manage by herself. Only Will Wittering was absent after their unexpected morning conversation.

Eight travelers filed into the inn and gathered round the table set for them with its spotless linen and gleaming flatware. A white-haired gentleman in clerical black and his thin, sharp-looking wife led the way, followed by a ginger-haired man with a yellow-dotted neckerchief, who smirked at Lucy. A pair who looked like farmers, and a sober, plain family, possibly Quakers, went straight to the table.

Lucy squared her shoulders and brought the soup round. Her guests prayed or began eating at once, as was their preference, except for the traveler with the ginger hair and loud neckcloth. He appeared to be in spirits and kept trying to snake an arm around Lucy's person at every opportunity.

As she brought the fish to the table and bent to lay it down, Hannah appeared at the foot of the stairs, signaling Lucy to come. Lucy nodded to Hannah and took her eye off the flashy gentleman. At the touch of his hand to her bottom, she jerked. Her platter tilted, and the pike slid from its nest of greens into the lap of the clergyman's wife.

There was an awful pause. Then the lady shrieked and jumped to her feet, dumping the fish to the floor, where it cast an accusing eye up at Lucy.

"You clumsy girl. You've ruined my gown." The woman held up her skirt with the wide wet imprint of the pike, like a dark grin pasted across her lap.

"I beg your pardon."

"You may be sure I'll report this episode to the coach company. I will be compensated."

Lucy drew herself up. "How much do you require?"

The guard entered and called for the passengers. The others stopped eating and began to gather cloaks and bundles, but the clergyman's wife dabbed at her ruined gown with a napkin.

"My dear," said the clergyman. "Come...."

"George, be quiet. I will be compensated for my gown before I take a step toward that stage."

"But the stage will go on without us. You won't want to stay the night in this inn."

"Certainly not."

The bench sitters began to murmur. "B'aint the thing to let Mrs. Vell go."

"Nothin' good can come of such a change."

Lucy retrieved her cash box and drew out a stack of Bank of England notes. The bench sitters hushed. There wasn't a person in the room who did not respect those notes. "How much?"

The woman's eyes narrowed. "Six pounds."

A low whistle came from the benches.

Lucy produced the notes without a blink. "Sign this receipt." She offered the woman a pen and paper, and the woman signed with a flourish.

"Don't think you've heard the end of this, girl." She swept out of the common room with her husband trailing after her.

Lucy stared at the pike. She had thought it would be easy to take charge. She felt the bench sitters watching, and judging. She could hear the continued murmur of commentary. She drew a steadying breath. First things first. The pike.

Queenie, the opportunist, padded over on silent feet, crouched down, and began to lick the pike's imprint from the floor. Lucy shooed the cat away and knelt on the flagstones with the empty platter. She slid a pair of serving spoons under the fish to lift it. The malevolent pike promptly broke into three pieces. She emptied the spoons full of broken fish onto the platter and started again while Queenie mewed and circled around behind her. An inconvenient ache made itself known low in Lucy's back. She resisted the urge to press her fish-coated hand against the place.

"Trouble, Miss Holbrook?" said a familiar voice.

"Nothing I can't handle, Captain Clare," she said without looking up.

His hand gripped her arm and lifted her from the floor. "Blodget, get your mistress some help," he ordered, his voice quiet but commanding.

"You..." she said, trying to frame some resistance to his interfering ways.

"I know. I'm giving orders again, and I will until you start giving some yourself."

He led her to Adam's bench, sat her down, and stood over her while Frank and Hannah dealt with the fish.

"Sorry about yer fish, miss," Hannah said as she passed with the pike's remains on her way to the kitchen. "It's all that gentleman's fault, too. He skipped, miss. That's wot I was trying to tell ye. I'm sorry."

"Not your fault, Hannah," Lucy replied. "Save some fish for Queenie." She looked up at Harry Clare. "Satisfied?"

"It's a start."

"Well, you won't like it if you teach me to give you orders."

"Depends on the orders you give me." He grinned, and she caught her breath at the change in his uncompromising face.

* * * *

Lucy Holbrook sat on the bench beside the sleeping Adam, the cat curled in her lap. It did not appear that they had moved since the incident with the fish. The old man looked so deep in sleep that Harry thought he could hazard a few of his questions.

"Your father's death upset him?"

She nodded, her fingers stroking the cat's white neck.

"Does he have a room or a bed somewhere?"

"He sleeps in Papa's room."

"Even now?" Harry could understand if Tom Holbrook had given the blind man a bed in the stable, but that Holbrook had kept Adam as close as family deepened the mystery.

"I... There's a chair. I keep watch."

"Not forever." Harry had a momentary desire to take hold of her slumping shoulders and shake her. It was a youthful mistake to think she could shoulder the burden of the inn and Adam.

"Until I can make some other arrangement."

Harry shook his head. "Wearing yourself out won't help Adam. Come on. Let me help you get him to bed. I can sit up with him tonight."

She looked up at him then, with more suspicion than gratitude. "You have no ties to Adam, no duty...."

"Let's say, I want my breakfast in the morning and need my innkeeper to take her rest." That was as much as he was willing to admit, but it gave her pause and made her take a longer look at him. He recognized that measuring gaze, the effort of a fighter to size up his opponent.

He knew what another man, a man like Richard, would see—a half-pay officer in a frayed and faded red coat, a man who'd seen action but not advancement, a down-and-out soldier, clinging to past glory. It was the disguise he had been wearing as a spy in all the low places where old soldiers gathered. He knew what some women would see in him, a hardness and a hunger that would be good to satisfy the itch created by conjugal sameness. He didn't know what an innocent like Lucy Holbrook would see.

He offered stare for stare, unyielding. It was a test of wills. Hers was strong, but weakened by grief and fatigue, she was no match for him. Her gaze dropped. "Thank you," she said. "Let me wake him. I know the trick of it."

Taking one of Adam's great hands in hers and speaking softly, Lucy coaxed the old man awake. He lifted his head and cocked it to one side, listening to the sounds of the inn, quiet now, with only Frank Blodget closing up in the tap.

"Who's there?" Adam asked hoarsely.

Lucy squeezed his hand. "It's me, Lucy, and Captain Clare. You've been sleeping. Let me take you to your proper bed. I've saved some pudding for you."

"Adam likes pudding." The old man turned with unerring instinct toward Harry. "You like pudding, Captain?"

"I do." The old man might make a better witness than Harry had imagined, if his other senses could supply the deficiency of his eyes.

"Adam," said Lucy, "put your left arm over Captain Clare's shoulder, and he will help you to Papa's room." She lifted the cat from her lap. The creature raised its tail and strutted off with offended dignity.

Harry moved next to Adam on the bench. When Adam's arms were positioned over their shoulders, Harry and Lucy rose, steadying the old man on his feet.

"Ready?" he asked.

She nodded, and they began to move toward the hall at the back of the inn.

At the last door in the hall, Lucy stopped and turned the latch. "Can you hold him up?" she asked. "We need a light."

"I can manage," Harry answered. Adam was a large, rawboned figure of a man, but there was little weight on his tall frame.

She slipped into the dark and lit a lamp. In its glow a man's room emerged with the inn's golden yellow walls and dark beams overhead. Harry understood at a glance how Adam Pickersgill had remained hidden from the world for twenty years. Under the stairs at the back of the inn, the room was a sanctuary. Two tall wardrobes stood opposite a large oak bed. A worn Turkey rug and a faded red velvet easy chair by the stone hearth gave color. Harry took note of drawers, books on a shelf, and a painted wooden box at the foot of the bed, all the places where a man stowed the things that mattered to him.

"Adam sleeps there." Lucy pointed.

Harry shifted his glance to a long low bed covered in a blue-and-white-striped rug tucked under the stairs. Together they maneuvered the old man to the edge of the bed, and he sank down.

Lucy turned promptly to Harry, in charge again. "Thank you, Captain."

"You're not finished with me yet," he told her. "Remember, I offered to sit with him tonight."

Her chin came up, and she shook her head. "Adam and I, we have a ritual." It was plain she did not want Harry intruding on a private moment. He bowed and withdrew. Tom Holbrook had gone to his grave with whatever secret made him hide Adam from the world. If any evidence remained of Adam's past, the dead man's room would be the first place to look for it. Harry would search her father's room as soon as he could.

*Through the ups and downs of the Season, the husband
hunter must keep her female friendships in good repair. She
must make time not only for morning calls, but also for visits of
compassion, commiseration, and shared joy. Furthermore, she
must keep up a regular correspondence with those friends from
whom she is, on occasion, separated. A letter full of the little
nothings of another's life is by its nature, in its trust and close
connection, restorative to the spirit. She will perhaps have few
friends to whom she may open her heart entirely, but the alert
female consciousness of a true friend is a powerful antidote to
errors of feeling. Alone, without female friends, the husband
hunter may come to depend on the attentions of gentlemen who
seek her company only to gratify their own vanity or lust.*

—The Husband Hunter's Guide to London

Chapter 5

A letter came from Margaret Leach in Wednesday's post. Her friends
had not abandoned her. Lucy tucked the letter in her pocket, promising
herself she'd read it the first chance she had. When she moved, the paper
made a noise, reminding her that it was there and reminding her of the lost
book, the gift her friends had given her. She'd asked Hannah and Ariel to
look for it, but neither of the girls had seen it.

The mystery of the lost book bothered her when she had time to think
of it, but most of the time she was simply too busy running between the
kitchen and the public room, or seeing to it that the girls kept at their tasks.
She was neglecting Adam, she knew, but once a day at least Captain Clare
sat with him, stroking the cat and talking the way Adam liked to talk about
ale and coffee and cats.

When she finally had a moment, she would read Margaret's letter and
do a thorough search for the book. It must be somewhere deep under
Adam's bench. She would take a broom handle and reach back to the wall.

The clang of metal hitting slate brought her from the kitchen on the run.
She swung around the tall back of Adam's black bench and saw Queenie,
her back arched high, hissing from the mantel. On the floor six brass
candlesticks rolled wildly, but no Adam sat on the bench.

Lucy glanced across the common room. At first she saw only the usual crowd of bench sitters with their pipes and mugs. Then her gaze found Adam. A man in a flat-brimmed hat and long coat had Adam by the arm and tugged him along toward the door.

"Adam," she called. "Stop. It's Lucy."

Adam halted and wheeled toward her voice, swinging the stranger, who clung to his arm, around to face her. "Adam stay." He planted his feet in a wide stance and tried to shake off the man's grip.

Lucy did not recognize the other man. She crossed the room with a quick stride. The bench sitters fell quiet. Face-to-face, the stranger was smaller than he first seemed. His clothes, from the wide-brimmed hat and greatcoat to the boots sagging about his ankles, looked too large for his frame. His face bristled with wild black brows and whiskers. His dark eyes were small and narrow in the pointed face of a burrowing creature. Lucy expected his sharp nose to twitch.

"Morning, miss," he said, drawing himself up. "I've come to collect your madman."

"Adam is not mad," Lucy corrected him. "And who are you?"

"I'm Findlater, miss, the new parish overseer. I heard that this fellow gave you a great deal of trouble on Sunday."

"Adam is not mad," Lucy repeated. "And he troubles no one, Mr. Findlater. I'm sorry you've come on a fruitless errand. I will take Adam back to his bench now."

Findlater shook his head. He had not let go of his hold on Adam's arm. Adam stood stiff and unmoving, his head cocked to one side.

"Now, miss, I don't want to quarrel with you, but this man doesn't belong here. He's not a St. Botolph's man at all. No record of him being dipped in the font, is there?"

"He's lived here for twenty years."

Findlater shook his head. "He ain't in the books, so to speak, ain't in the parish registry. He's a vagrant is what he is, miss. He must go to his own parish if he needs alms. He can't be taking food out of the mouths of St. Botolph's people."

"You're misinformed, Mr. Findlater, if you think Adam depends on parish charity. Adam earns his keep. He has been employed at the inn for years and makes it his home."

"Begging your pardon, miss, he's a public nuisance. Look where I found him—halfway to the door. Can't let his sort wander the high street. He needs minding. If you can't do it, miss, they'll do for him in the madhouse." Findlater looked at her pinny with its stains of gravy and currant jelly.

"No. Adam stays. He lives here. The inn people will look out for him."
Lucy looked around for Frank Blodget in the tap, but he wasn't there. No
one in the common room met her eye.

Findlater smirked.

The front door opened, and in strode Harry Clare. He shed his coat and
hat before he saw her then stopped, looking down on the scene, his scarlet
jacket bright in the late afternoon gloom. The bench sitters called out to
him, and Findlater turned for a moment.

Lucy took advantage of the distraction the captain made to step forward
and reach for Adam's left hand, taking it in hers and pulling gently. Adam's
hand shook in Lucy's. "I'm responsible for Adam. I'll see to him," she
told Findlater.

"Not so fast, miss. How can you mind him and keep the inn? Supposing
yer madman slips out while you're putting on the supper? Supposing he
has one of his fits and does a mischief to a passenger? How's Sir Geoffrey
to like that, eh?"

Lucy wanted to say that such a thing could never happen. A brief thought
crossed her mind at Findlater's reference to putting supper on for the stage
passengers. She did not recognize the man but wondered if he had been
there or had heard about the incident. "I will take all precautions."

"Trouble, Miss Holbrook?" Harry Clare's voice caused the parish
overseer to twist and look over his shoulder. He still had a hand on Adam's
arm.

The captain came down the three wide steps with an unhurried stride.
He stopped between Findlater and the stairs a couple of feet from Adam
and his would-be abductor. For a moment the two men looked at each
other. The captain's height and breadth of shoulder put a distinct obstacle
in Findlater's path.

Findlater cleared his throat. "And you are?"

"Captain Clare, a friend of Adam's. If Miss Holbrook takes responsibility
for Adam, your work is done. Best to go on about your other duties."

Again Findlater shook his head. "Now, Captain. You know I'm just doing
my job. I can't be making exceptions for pretty misses and the gentlemen
what are sweet on them."

"New to your job, aren't you? Who pointed out Adam to you?"

Findlater's gaze shifted. "Nobody tells Obadiah Findlater his duty."

"Someone did. Someone told you to come after Adam. Who set you
after a harmless old man minding his own work?"

Findlater glanced around at the onlookers and shifted from one foot to the other, tightening his grip on Adam. He thrust out his chin. "No one set me onto him. Just doing my duty as every man must."

"Consider it done then, and let Adam return to his work. Unless you want to explain your sudden interest in Adam to his friends here at the inn." Harry Clare nodded to the bench sitters.

"Here, here, Captain," cried a voice from the crowd.

For a moment Findlater wavered. Lucy thought his nose actually did twitch. He looked past the captain toward the door. He looked at the bench sitters. Then he flung Adam's arm aside and strode off. As the door banged shut behind him, a cheer went up and pint pots thumped the tables.

Lucy took Adam by the hand and led him back to his bench. She settled him there with his polish pot and his rags. Queenie jumped down from the mantel and brushed against Adam's leg, and he reached a hand down to stroke the cat's back. Lucy picked up the fallen candlesticks, conscious of laughter and talk from the bench sitters, who seemed to hail Harry's victory over Findlater as their own, and in which the captain's voice sounded a deeper, more subdued note. The smell of burnt sugar coming from the kitchen made her squeeze Adam's shoulder and dash for the cake she had left in the oven.

* * * *

Harry momentarily considered the usefulness of a partner like Nate Wilde. It would be easy for the youth to slip out after Findlater and trail the man to wherever he went to report on his failure. Harry waited for the laughter at Findlater's expense to subside. When the conversation returned to its usual topics, he went in search of Lucy.

"Findlater will be back, you know. A man like him doesn't forget a public humiliation. And whoever put him up to going after Adam won't be satisfied with today's result."

"What do you mean 'whoever put him up to it'?"

"Did it never occur to you that your father was hiding Adam?"

"From whom?"

"From whoever harmed him, blinded him."

"But that was long ago. Adam has lived here in peace for twenty years. Why would that change now?"

"Are you sure that when Adam cries out in his distress that what he says is meaningless?"

"You ask hard questions, Captain."

"You want to protect him, don't you?"

"But Adam goes nowhere, and no one in the inn means him any harm. They may laugh, but they are used to Adam's ways. Oh, you mean a stranger."

"Think. Did anyone new see Adam's outburst on Sunday?"

"Now you are insulting. My friends are ladies, and they would not involve themselves with someone like Findlater."

"Someone did."

She appeared to consider it. "There was a guest Monday who skipped, a gentleman, Hannah said. He ordered the fish, but left without eating or paying."

* * * *

It was late when Harry returned to the inn. A few lamps remained lit. The doors and shutters had not yet been closed. Lucy and Adam occupied the usual bench at the back of the common room. Adam leaned against the tall back of the bench, his mouth slightly open, his breathing regular, the cat curled in his lap. Lucy slumped forward onto the table, her head resting on an open ledger. The cook's desertion had helped Harry's cause by exhausting the girl.

He closed a fist around the keys hanging from a brass ring at her waist and cut the ring free of its ribbon tie. The cat blinked at him, but neither the girl nor the old man stirred. Harry summoned Hannah the maid.

He handed the sleepy girl Lucy's keys. "Open your mistress's door, put a lamp on in her room, and report back to me."

Hannah blinked at him, but turned to do as he'd asked.

Harry stood for a minute listening to her tread on the stairs. Somewhere above the guest chambers were smaller rooms for maids and one for Lucy herself. He'd spent more than a fortnight trying not to think about Lucy Holbrook's bed. Now it was his duty to place her in it. He grinned. Not all duties were unpleasant.

Hannah returned with a curtsy and the keys. Harry gave her a coin for her trouble, which brightened her look. "Are you ready for your next assignment?" he asked.

She nodded.

"Good. I'm putting you on sentry duty. You're to sit with Adam on his bench while I take Miss Holbrook up to her room. Can you do it?"

Hannah glanced warily at the sleeping Adam and swallowed. She looked as uncertain as the rawest recruit hearing big guns for the first time. At last she nodded.

"You can do it, Hannah. A quarter of an hour, no more."

She put her coin in a pocket and settled on the bench beside Adam. Harry turned to Lucy. What little light glowed from a few candles and a low fire seemed to find her golden head and make it shine.

An effective officer is an efficient officer. Harry repeated the line to himself as he lifted her arms and head from the table, swung her feet to the floor, and caught her up in his arms, her head resting against his chest. She was as curved and soft and warm and womanly as he'd guessed from his stolen glances of her across the inn. The scent of her hair and skin made his head swim briefly.

Harry had moved wagons up mountainsides in the mud. He had moved horses across rocky gorges of rushing streams. He had moved men forward in the face of withering French fire. Now he had only to move one sleeping woman to her bed.

He repeated the line about efficiency many times as he made his way up two flights of stairs to her room. The door was open, and Hannah's lamp on the mantel illuminated a small, neat room, softened by feminine touches. He lowered them onto the canopied bed with its virginal muslin hangings.

He settled the girl on his lap, leaning her forward against one arm, so that he could work the buttons on the back of her gown. The tiny buttons covered in the fine black wool of the gown and the weight of soft breasts against his arm and bottom in his lap interfered with the steadiness of his fingers.

"Almost there," he whispered to the girl as he spread the sides of the gown, pushing it down off her shoulders.

It stymied him a moment that her stays closed in the front. She was a practical woman, after all, not a fine lady with a maid to lace her up. So he stood and turned and laid her out on the bed. He looked down at the sleeping girl, but he wasn't about to retreat now with the job half done. With sudden efficiency, he lifted her skirts, dispensed with her shoes, pulled the black gown down over her hips and legs, untied her petticoats and stripped them away, too.

Now she lay before him in plain fine cotton so sheer it gave the illusion of a mere veil over the sweet soft curves and shadows of her that he wanted to touch. His twelve years of soldiering had come to nothing more than a few relics in a glass case, yet he did not regret his time in the army. Whatever the harsh lessons of war, the army had also refined his senses, taught him nuances. He had learned to quiet every competing thought so that he might suck the pleasure from a rare moment of peace, like watching a sleeping girl.

But Tom Holbrook's solid bulk no longer stood between Lucy and himself, so he took a step back from the bed, tossed her discarded garments on a chair by the hearth, and allowed himself one last look before he drew the white counterpane over the sleeping girl.

He turned to put out the lamp and saw the portrait of a picnicking lady on the wall above the small hearth. Even in the dim light of a single lamp, the portrait was striking in its overlarge size and its subject, surely remote from the girl. Harry did not recognize the lady, but he was sure he knew the house, that he'd been to that house, in his youth, perhaps when he was thirteen or so and tagging after Richard on some shooting expedition. The name of the place would come to him. He put out the lamp. His mission, for better or worse, was to get the old man's information. So he would leave Lucy Holbrook to her dreams and rouse tall, lanky Adam and help him through his nighttime ritual. He shut the door and descended the stairs.

He found Hannah awake and edgy. He thanked her, gave her a coin for her trouble, and sent her off to bed.

He put a hand on Adam's shoulder and spoke to him as Lucy would. After a minute the old man stirred, and Queenie jumped from his lap.

"You like cats very much," Adam said to him.

"I do," said Harry. "Let's get you to bed, Adam."

Harry helped Adam to his feet, put the old man's hand on his shoulder, and turned them toward the passageway to Tom Holbrook's room.

Together they shuffled down the passageway. Harry used Lucy's key to open the door and made Adam stand in the doorway while Harry lit a lamp, conscious of how easy it was for him to go from darkness to light, how the room sprang into view at the flaring of the wick, while nothing changed for the old man.

Adam talked of Tom Holbrook while Harry helped the old man remove his clothes and shoes and put on a long nightshirt. The old man's slow deliberate attention to each step of the process allowed Harry to study the room again. If Tom Holbrook had kept any clues to Adam's past, a likely place was the locked bottom drawer of the wardrobe.

"Mr. Tom dead?" Adam asked.

"He is," Harry agreed.

"Tonight, Captain Clare guard?" The old man's voice was worried.

"Yes, Adam. I guard." Harry thought it an odd choice of word, even for the old man. It was a word that implied a threat.

When at last Adam had stretched out on the bed under the stairs, Harry helped him pull the rug up over him and settled in the armchair. He envied Adam Pickersgill his apparently dreamless sleep. Whatever troubled the man's waking mind from time to time in such a terrible way left his unconscious undisturbed. There was no movement from Adam's bed except the regular rise and fall of his chest with his breathing. He lay as peaceful as a child.

Harry rose from the chair and lit a second lamp, positioning it to illuminate the tall wardrobe with its upper cabinet and lower drawers. There was no mystery in the cabinet, in shirts and coats hanging in neat array. Nor was there anything in the first drawer of the wardrobe but smalls and stockings, gloves and woolen scarves.

If the wardrobe held any information about Adam, it would be in the locked lower drawer. With a bit of guesswork and bit of luck, Harry was able to turn a key in the lock on the third try. The drawer stuck a bit from being full, and Harry worked patiently to pull it out only far enough to examine the contents. The drawer emitted a musty smell of cedar and old things, things that had not breathed in a long time.

On the surface of it, the drawer appeared to hold a jumble of unrelated clothes and books, and yet there was a neat order to the arrangement that spoke of a deliberate effort to preserve the items collected. On the left he found a girl's sampler in threads of yellow, blue, and green; a child's slate; and a bundle of letters tied with a cord. The items must have belonged to Lucy and not the old man, who had never learned to read or write. Harry paused and looked around the room for some other likely place where Tom Holbrook might have kept something of Adam's past.

Nothing else possessed a lock. Harry turned back to the drawer.

He made a note of the arrangement of items and carefully lifted each one from the drawer. Beneath the letter bundle he found an old edition of the peerage, an item that could not have belonged to Lucy. He lifted the book out of its nest of garments and read the date inside the cover. If he looked, he would find his father's name, and his and Richard's. Richard's words about being a dead branch of the family tree came back to him. He thumbed the book for any hint of Tom Holbrook's reason for keeping it, and it fell open to a page turned down. The entry on two facing pages read:

LYDFORD of Hartwood Park

Edward Lydford, born May 2, 1754, married September 4, 1779, Lady Charlotte Longshaw, daughter of Nicholas

*Longshaw, by which lady he has issue Penelope, born April 7,
1780; John, January 22, 1782; Henry, November 16, 1785.*

*Principal seat, Hartwood Park in the county of Leicester.
Heir presumptive: John Nicholas Lydford*

As soon as he saw the name, he knew Hartwood was the house in
the portrait in Lucy's room. Hartwood Park was not fifteen miles from
Mountjoy. Harry wondered whether John Lydford was still their neighbor.
Harry had been allowed to come along one winter when John invited
Richard to a shooting party at Hartwood. Penelope Lydford was then
being courted in London as a great beauty. Her brother told them with
some disgust that his sister was mad for a French count.

Harry closed the book. Lucy's comment that she thought Adam had
been in service came back to him, but if Tom Holbrook had discovered
that Adam came from Hartwood Park, why had he not sent Adam back
there? Harry set the book on the rug and reached down into the next
layer of items in the drawer. He found a child's primer, a book about the
adventures of a boy named Tom True accompanied by his friend Prudence,
and a box of pencils and chalks. At the very bottom of the drawer was a
soft bundle wrapped in thin yellowing crepe. He lifted it out of the drawer
and unwrapped the bundle.

On top of the bundle lay a girl child's white lace cap with one broken
string and a single white knitted mitten for a tiny hand. Beneath the lace
cap and mitten was a muslin gown also for a young girl. Fine embroidery
circled the neck of the gown and continued down the center panel. It was
a gown fit for a young princess, but when Harry lifted it, the folds of the
gown fell away, and a long brown stain appeared from the center of the
gown down to its hem. The stain was one he knew well. He'd buried men
who wore that stain on their clothes, but he had never seen it on a child's
garment. He lay the gown aside and looked at the last item in the bundle,
a pale blue wool child's coat with knotted silk embroidery to match the
gown, and a blood stain every bit as deep and dark.

*Inevitably as the husband hunter prepares for the Season,
she thinks first of its delights. She anticipates the thrill of
dancing with a desirable partner and the pleasure of a
handsome gentleman's attentions. She is certain of being ready
for such happy occasions. But our English weather should
teach her to prepare equally for those less happy moments,
which are part of every husband hunter's experience, moments
of distress and awkwardness. The most distressing forms of
awkwardness arise whenever there is an unequal degree of
admiration and regard between two persons. When the husband
hunter observes a gentleman, to whom she has made her
interest plain, choose another, or when she must meet again
a man whom she has refused as a partner in the dance or in
life, she must exercise the greatest degree of self-mastery. She
must not permit herself to blush. Rather she must exert herself
to put the other person at ease. Once she has done so, she will
discover how readily her own comfort and hopes are restored.*

—The Husband Hunter's Guide to London

Chapter 6

Lucy woke early to sun streaming in her window. She was in her room
in her bed, but not in her nightgown or between the sheets. Her brush and
comb lay on the chest, and her lady's portrait hung over the mantel in the
most ordinary and familiar way. She simply couldn't remember going to
bed. Her gaze drifted to her clothes lying discarded in a heap on her chair
and Margaret's letter lying on the carpet. The present rushed back, and she
was throwing off the counterpane, her feet slapping the floor, and Papa
was dying, dead, and buried, and she had the inn to run and Adam to care
for. She had slipped back in time while she slept to before, but waking had
borne her swiftly into the present like a twig tossed in a swollen stream.

It was already too bright out, and the birds' morning chorus had quieted.
She hurried through her washing and dressing. It troubled her that she
could not remember climbing to her room or undressing. Worse, she had
abandoned Adam. Unthinkable that she had done so. She did not remember
helping him to bed. He could not have gone on his own. With the briefest
nod to her smiling lady, she ran down the stairs.

Adam was not on his bench, but Queenie jumped down and meowed, loudly demanding breakfast. Lucy made herself stand and think while the cat wound around her legs. A night's sleep should not have altered things so completely as if she'd entered a dark wood and lost her bearings. Queenie's cries grew more insistent, and Lucy headed for the kitchen. *Feed the cat. Find Adam. And the world would right itself.* She quickened her step at the sound of Hannah's voice and found her at the long kitchen worktable arranging a teapot and covered dish on a silver tray. The girl looked up and bobbed a curtsy and offered a good morning as if nothing were amiss.

"Morning, Hannah." Lucy filled the cat's dish with the fish scraps Queenie preferred. Once the cat stopped mewing, Lucy could think. She had merely overslept. "Adam's not on his bench." It was an odd thing to say, like saying the earth is flat. "Do you know where he is?"

Hannah looked down with a slight blush. "Don'cha remember, miss? Captain Clare did for 'im last night. After he did for you. I expect 'e's with the captain in 'is room."

After he did for you. He did for her? Lucy did not remember. Why did she not remember? "Thank you, Hannah. Carry on."

She left the girls in the kitchen and marched up the stairs and down the passage to the captain's corner bedchamber, sentences forming in her head. She would tell Captain Clare what she thought of a man interfering with her running of the inn. He had one of the inn's finest rooms, with its half-tester bed and a view over the meadows beyond their little village at the edge of London. At his door she reached for the keys at her waist, found them missing. She rapped sharply on the heavy door.

"Come in," a muffled male voice called.

When she pushed open the door, her complaint died. Captain Clare stood with his back to her, his back bare, with a towel draped over one pale broad shoulder, his left hand holding a razor to his jaw. Once before she'd had an encounter with him when he'd first come to the inn. She hadn't realized which room her father had given him and had opened the door to discover him lying in the copper bath.

Whatever she meant to say about his interference with Adam died in her suddenly dry throat. His shoulders needed no epaulets. They were quite broad. His smooth skin was marked by tiny white nicks, and one long, thin red line that slashed from under his right shoulder blade down to the band of his trousers.

Heat shimmered in the lazy gaze that collided with hers in the glass. The meaning of Hannah's words came clear and robbed Lucy of speech.

"You." His raised hand paused in its scraping of the lather on his chin, like a clock figure waiting for the next second to tick off. Then he shook the foam from the blade into the white, chipped basin in front of him. "Come to scold, have you? Adam's safe."

Lucy bowed her head to hide her flaming cheeks. Harry Clare had undressed her and put her to bed. His hands had touched her where no one touched her. Her whole body flashed with sudden warmth at the thought. She tried to tell herself that his attentions must have been swift and impersonal, or at the least not...not other than her care of Adam.

She had forgotten Adam, but there he was in a chair by the fire, dressed and combed, his hands resting on his knees, his head cocked at an alert angle. She crossed the Turkey rug to rest a hand on his shoulder.

"How are you this morning, Adam?" she asked.

"Captain Clare takes a bath every day," said Adam. "He likes baths."

Lucy's face warmed again. A slight shiver passed through her. She stood where the copper bath stood. In that moment he had lain in the tub, his arms resting over the edges, his hands with their long fingers dangling, his head tilted back against the lip, his eyes closed, water beaded on his shoulders, steam rising around him.

"You undressed me," she said, putting it plainly, sounding him out.

He glanced at her again over his shoulder. "I'm sure you'd return the favor if I needed it."

"Favor?" The image of him in the tub remained vivid in her mind. He filled her with vast impatience, she who had patiently cared for Adam for years.

"I hope you slept well. Adam did." He tossed the towel aside and reached for a shirt lying on the end of the bed. He pulled it over his head, and the loose lawn fell into place, shadowing his torso. He had seen her in a similar state.

He fastened the cuffs of the shirt. She ought to be glad he was decent. The conversation had veered away from her complaint, and she sought to bring it back. "Adam is my responsibility."

"Along with everything else, apparently."

"Yes, and I'll thank you to return my keys."

"Such a lot of brass to carry. You must feel the weight of them with every step."

"I can manage. You think I'm not up to running an inn."

He shook his head. "You needed sleep, not another night of watching over Adam." From the table by the bed he gathered up her ring of keys, hefting them in his palm and handing them to her. Their fingers met with a brief shock.

Lucy went to tie the keys to her waist, but found the ribbon had been cut. She dropped them in her pocket, where they made a heavy bulge. When she looked up, she saw her missing book lying on the table beside the bed.

"You took my book, the book my friends gave me."

"You left it behind. You'd better read it, you know." He picked up his scarlet regimental jacket from the end of the bed.

She laughed. "I'm not likely to hunt a husband any time soon."

Lucy watched him shrug into the jacket. She had dressed Adam countless times and never thought about shoulders or backs or waists. "Don't you have ordinary clothes?" The war was long over, yet he still wore his uniform, and under it his scars. "Is England at war?"

"She still has enemies." He smiled grimly.

"And you fight them?"

"Every day." He shrugged. The scarlet coat hung loose around him. The shirt hung over his trousers. Lucy felt oddly rooted to the carpet and realized he was waiting for her to leave. She had things to do, whatever he thought of a woman's capacity to manage an inn.

"I'll take my book, thank you."

He moved with lazy ease to retrieve it and hand it to her. This time there was no meeting of their fingers. "You have more neighbors nerving themselves to propose, you know."

"Propose? To me? Who?"

"You turned Wittering down, but John Simkins will have a go at it. You're a woman of property. Fair game. You haven't noticed the new coats and combed hair?"

She dropped the little book in her other pocket—it was far lighter than her keys—and turned to Adam. She squeezed his hand once, a signal they had when it was time to move from one spot to another. Adam tottered to his feet, and Lucy led him to the door.

"Thank you, Captain," she said, "for seeing to Adam last night."

"My pleasure," he said as she and Adam passed through the door.

Lucy looked back, unable to help herself. He hadn't moved, and his face had its hardest look. "Your father protected Adam, kept him from being noticed, pretended that what Adam says makes no sense, but what if it does make sense? What if Adam knows a secret that could bring him... and you great harm?"

* * * *

Harry breakfasted in the common room over an ordnance survey map of Berkshire and Buckinghamshire. Studying the map should help him clear his head after his morning encounter with Lucy Holbrook. He had no quarrel with the Tooth and Nail's eggs and toast, but his cup of undrinkable inn coffee cooled as he studied the map for likely ambush sites. A number of details puzzled Harry about Adam's past.

If Lucy's account were accurate and Adam had been in service, and if, as Tom Holbrook's marked copy of the peerage suggested, Adam had been employed at Hartwood Park, then the attack would likely have occurred on the Aylesbury-to-London road, a road Harry had often ridden between Mountjoy and town. It was the route Radcliffe's Rockets followed.

Supposing Adam had been attacked and blinded somewhere within walking distance of the inn, which Harry thought to be five to eight miles for a man of Adam's strength, there were a few likely ambush spots where the road passed through woods or open heath.

But what he knew of the attack still made no sense. A man in service would have been traveling with a master or mistress and at least a coachman, if not other servants. If a child had been present, the party would likely have included the mistress of the house and a nursemaid. So how had Adam alone ended up at the inn? What had become of the child whose bloody garments lay in Tom Holbrook's wardrobe?

At the time, the master of Hartwood had been the Clares' neighbor, Edward Lydford, whose offspring were closer in age to Harry's brother, Richard, than to Harry, two sons and a daughter. As far as Harry knew, Lydford, a man in his seventies, still held the title; his eldest son was betrothed or married, but Harry did not remember what had become of the other two Lydford children. Harry knew of no child belonging to the family twenty years earlier. He had been thirteen at the time.

The answers to the puzzle lay locked away in Adam's disordered mind. Ordinarily, when Harry and his fellow spies wanted information out of an informant, they'd take the fellow to the nearest public house and keep the drinks coming until the man opened up. He could not treat Adam that way. The old man sat all day in a busy taproom, but no amount of drink would loosen his tongue. Apparently, only a reminder of his blinding could make him talk. As tempting as it was to put those bloody garments in Adam's big rough hands and ask him direct questions, Harry had no intention of harming Adam or further scattering his wits. To get Adam to talk, Harry was going to have to win Lucy's cooperation.

And while he tried to get the girl on his side, his brother, Richard, could sell Mountjoy out from under him before the government ever paid him a shilling of what he was owed for his year and a day as a spy. He lifted the cold coffee to his mouth and put it down again. The problem was charming Lucy Holbrook. Harry was no Hazelwood with an easy, engaging manner or a playful way with words. His uniform was apparently distasteful to her. He'd only been in London for a few weeks one Season when he'd returned briefly from the Peninsula to recover from a wound. Maybe he should have read her little book before he'd returned it to her.

He pushed the cold coffee away, laughing at himself. Whenever he let himself think about Lucy, he stopped thinking straight. He was a soldier with a mission. He needed to ride out and find the likely place of the ambush. Reconstructing the crime would be the first step toward understanding Adam's disjointed ravings.

Harry looked at his watch. The stage was past due, and Lucy remained in her kitchen preparing for its arrival. He suspected her of hiding from him after their earlier encounter in his room. Without her cook, the duty of preparing a meal for the stage passengers fell on her. He would stay until she got over that hurdle.

He folded his map, aware suddenly of the distinctive aroma of fresh strong coffee somewhere near him. He looked around the common room for one of Lucy's serving girls, but there was only the usual crowd of bench sitters, now gathered to see the drama of Lucy's managing the stage passengers. His gaze found a man in a familiar cap hunched over his drink at the far end of one of the benches. As if aware of Harry's scrutiny, the fellow in the cap turned.

Nate Wilde flashed his toothy grin and lifted a leather-coated flask in a salute.

Harry nodded, and the youth slid from his bench and crossed the room, putting the flask down at Harry's side. "Thought you might need some decent coffee, guv."

"Whelp, what are you doing here?"

"The big man sent me." Wilde slid onto the bench beside Harry. "And?"

"He thinks you might need help." Wilde opened the flask, and the full rich scent of the coffee hit Harry.

He wanted to say that he worked alone, but a look at the youth stopped him. Wilde was buzzing with pent-up energy. "Feeling idle?"

"Useless. Do you know Will Jones employs a fellow that will turn down your sheets for you and...and more?" Wilde grinned, all his strong, white teeth in view.

Harry laughed. In some ways he and the youth were alike. Both had fended for themselves for years, Wilde in a bleak, lawless London rookery, and Harry at war.

"Is that your blind man?" Wilde asked, looking across the inn at Adam on his bench.

"Yes." Harry took his first taste of Wilde's coffee, rich and strong. "What do you see?" An early occupation of picking pockets had taught Wilde to be a sharp observer of people. Harry enjoyed a few more swallows of the coffee while the youth studied Adam, who was buffing a pair of boots.

"I see the cat, sir. The cat's not moving. I'd say the old man sticks to his business as long as the cat sleeps. When the cat stirs, the old man will prick up his ears. There's nothing wrong with his hearing, is there?"

"Nothing." Harry thought it a good performance for a man trying to win a place on the case, and maybe Harry could use him. He could certainly use the coffee. He'd think it over.

The inn bell jangled, and the door blew open. Every head turned to the entrance. In walked King Cole, the most notable coachman of Radcliffe's Rockets. His flushed and angry face, his muddied boots, proclaimed trouble. Then he started shouting.

"Holbrook! Where are ye, man? Call the constables, damn ye! My Rocket's been robbed again." Cole strode straight to the tap. Blodget handed him a pint, which he downed in a single drink. The bench sitters left their benches to gather around him, a jumble of shouting voices.

Harry kept his gaze on Adam. The cat had left the bench, and the old man sat in a strained frozen posture, his hands still, his head cocked to listen to the din from the tap.

Lucy came running from the kitchen, checking only to put a hand on Adam's shoulder before striding up to Cole.

"Mr. Cole, what's happened? Where are your passengers?"

Cole looked surprised to be addressed by her. Harry watched the man's face change as he took in the keys Lucy had retied to her waist.

"They shot out the lamps at the seven-mile stone. Got my guard, Fishlock, too. And took the bleeding 'orses." He reached for another cup of ale.

"Who?" someone from the crowd asked.

"Gypsies. Spoke gibberish, the lot of them, except the leader. Big fellow on a black horse."

"Mr. Cole," Lucy interrupted. "Is anyone hurt?"

Cole frowned at her. "Had to leave the passengers, miss. No 'orses."

Lucy turned and strode for the door. Harry nudged Wilde. "Go help her. Get the stable master to collect the passengers."

Wilde was up off the bench and at Lucy's side before she reached the door. Harry heard him calling, "Miss," saw them talk, and Wilde hurry out the door. Lucy turned back, watching Cole.

Harry stood and crossed to Adam's side, settling beside the old man. "King Cole is telling a story, Adam. Lucy's listening." The cat jumped into Harry's lap, and he shifted the creature over to Adam to hold. The old man's hands curled around the animal.

Cole was on his third pint, telling the story of the encounter at a place where the road curved around a low rise and ancient pollard beeches cast a deep gloom. The highwayman, whoever he was, had worn no lace or plume. No silver had glinted from his weapon, and the dark brim of his hat had hidden his features. Adding insult to injury, the fellow had taken Cole's whip and tommy, a short murderous weapon of weighted whalebone that could make the slowest horse give a faster mile.

Harry did not have to consult his map to know that the place Cole described was one Harry had already identified as a good place for an ambush. He placed a hand on Adam's shaking knee. The old man was muttering, "Geoffrey ran away."

"Steady, Adam. Lucy's safe." It was a guess, a stab in the dark, but the muttering stopped. "Lucy's here. She's safe," Harry repeated.

Adam quieted, still holding his head cocked in a listening attitude. His right hand stroked the cat. Queenie purred and began to knead Adam's leg with her claws.

A constable arrived, and Lucy led him and Cole to the inn's private parlor. The bench sitters continued to talk about the robbery, speculating about the odd behavior of the thieves in taking Radcliffe's horses. Everyone knew Radcliffe's night-run horses were on their last legs and apt to die in the traces, especially with a coachman like Cole driving them.

Only Lucy's passage back across the common room to Adam's bench created a brief pause in the talk. Every man took a moment to lift his pint pot again. While they were drinking, Wilde slipped back into the crowd, a pair of eyes and ears Harry could count on.

Lucy came straight to Adam's bench and sat on the old man's other side, speaking quietly, assuring him that no one had been seriously hurt, not even Fishlock the wounded guard, telling him that a wagon had been sent to collect the passengers. Harry watched Adam grow easy under the influence of the girl's sweet, steady voice.

"We must thank Captain Clare," she told Adam, "for sitting with you. I'm sure it helped to have a friend at your side."

Adam nodded. "Captain Clare likes cats," he said. "Captain Clare does not run away."

A brief alarm flashed in the girl's eyes at the reference to running away. The key to the old man's distress lay in that act of someone's running away. Years ago someone had bolted in a confrontation on the road. Harry's next duty was to find the spot where the terrible event occurred. He would start by looking at the place where bandits had stopped the Radcliffe Rocket. And he had an idea of how he could use Wilde's help after all.

* * * *

For the moment Harry had a partner. He would take Wilde with him to the scene of the ambush, and then send the youth off to investigate Adam's past.

As partners went, Wilde was not too bad, but he was London-bred, and though game for anything, he was no rider, so Harry took a gig from the inn stables. He wanted to reach the abandoned coach ahead of the constable and before a fresh team arrived to move the vehicle.

A wet, snowy March had given way to a bright, dry day. The budding trees wore a hint of spring color, and only the wheel ruts shone with traces of rainwater. They passed the inn wagon bringing the passengers and the wounded guard back, and it occurred to Harry that Cole wasn't a man to be in charge of anything. Cole had left the coach behind, and surely, Radcliffe expected his employees to guard his property. At the four-mile stone they passed the last cottages of St. Botolph's and left the outskirts of London behind. The landscape changed to open rolling heath with stands of trees and clumps of dense foliage. Beside Harry, Wilde grew more alert.

"Looks like plenty of places for an ambush," he said.

Harry nodded. At night, too, the coach on the road with its lamps lit would make quite a target for anyone concealed in the darkness of trees or bush, but Harry thought the place wasn't right yet, still too close to civilization, and with a well-marked, open road to tempt a bold coachman like Cole to try to outrun his assailants.

As they approached the seven-mile stone, the landscape changed again. Pollard beeches grew close to the road, their branches intertwining overhead, and the road itself narrowed and disappeared around a low rise. When they rounded the bend, they found the abandoned coach square in the middle of the road. A track split off to their right into the woods. Harry could see at once why thieves had chosen the spot. The curve of the road, the uphill slope on one side, and the close proximity of trees and bush would slow the coach's progress and momentarily cut it off in either direction from help or escape.

He turned the inn gig into the wood and halted under a stand of trees. Wilde jumped down and walked toward the coach. "Perfect spot for a lay, sir, but what kind of thief takes near-dead horses and not the passengers' fat purses? Seems a queer thing to me. From what I heard in the tap, there were several in the gang, but they mostly ignored the passengers. The leader knew Cole, I think."

"One of them had experience working with teams to do the unhitching rapidly," Harry commented.

"Right," said Wilde. "So not your usual thieves."

Harry agreed. Horses on the night run for Radcliffe's Rockets would be in the last weeks or months of their lives. Most of them would die in harness. And, as Wilde pointed out, it made no sense to ignore the potential treasure of the passengers' purses or the gold that Sir Geoffrey was reported to ship.

Harry felt he was missing something. The road made a perfect Y. From where he stood at the foot of that Y, a man could dominate the scene in front of him, while to his right the track into the woods offered an easy escape route. Someone had carefully chosen the spot but had taken the thing that had the least value. What had the robbers gained by what they did? A thrush landed on the coach box, let out a burst of song, looked at Harry, and took off again. *Unless the point was just that—to separate the passengers from the coach.* Only this time, the passengers had stayed put for hours.

"Wilde, search inside."

The youth scrambled up into the coach. "What am I looking for?"

"Concealed compartments."

Harry turned off the main road down the right branch of the Y and followed it deeper into the wood. He didn't want to jump to conclusions, but he had the strongest feeling that the spot had been used before by thieves and perhaps by one murderer. Someone had swept the track with tree branches, but the scent of lathered horses lingered in the air, and scattered droppings lay in the dead leaves at the side of the track.

A few paces farther on, a deep hoofprint in the soft ground at the edge of the track made Harry stop to examine the brush. At a broken place in the screen of foliage he pushed his way into a wide clearing. The muddied ground had been trampled by hooves, and a fresh pile of dung attracted flies. The thieves had been quick but not entirely thorough. A shaft of sunlight flashed on something on the ground. With his boot he nudged a low branch aside and found a bit of steel from the horses' discarded harness. He scanned the clearing. Nothing more appeared.

The place was quiet, and even Harry had to admit that it was lovely, better suited for a lovers' meeting than a murder. He was daft to think it might be the place of the attack on Adam years earlier, but his instinct for danger held him there. If there were a connection, the violence of that earlier attack would have left its mark on the scene. He broke off a stout branch and circled the clearing, pushing aside the undergrowth and stirring up the dead leaves.

He was halfway around the clearing when his stick turned up something. He bent down and pulled it free of the low branch on which it was snagged. It was a mitten for a hand that would fit in Harry's palm.

He was thinking about the mitten's mate lying in Tom Holbrook's drawer when he heard Wilde calling his name.

"Over here," he yelled.

"Found something, sir," Wilde replied. "Where are you?"

"Push through the brush. You'll find a clearing."

Wilde came crashing through, triumphantly holding a scrap of paper aloft in one hand. "You were right, sir. Concealed compartments all over the coach. Two beneath the forward-facing seats, and two behind the rear-facing ones. This bit was caught in the corner."

Harry took the torn triangle of paper. It looked to be the lower corner of a letter with a portion of the signature intact. The letters *twell* appeared in a stiff formal script that Harry knew well.

"What does it mean, sir?" Wilde asked.

"It's Chartwell's signature," Harry said. Chartwell was the source of the spies' funding. It was he who had shut down their operation. Someone was stealing documents from under Chartwell's nose. Harry tucked the scrap of paper into his jacket and clapped the lad on the shoulder. "It means I have two jobs for you. Are you game to ride the night run of Radcliffe's Rockets?"

Wilde nodded.

"Good. We need to find out who's using the Rockets to smuggle Foreign Office documents out of London." He led the way back through the hazel screen to the road.

As they climbed back into the gig, Wilde asked, "What's the other job?"

"You're to go to Hartwood to find out everything you can about our blind man. He was in service there once."

Harry turned the gig back toward the inn. He was thinking about how to approach Chartwell when he became aware of the intensity of Wilde's silence. The whelp was also deep in thought.

"What?" Harry asked.

"A man needs a partner, sir. Can I take Miranda with me?"

Harry shrugged. "All the same to me."

A vexing question the husband hunter may face is whether to allow a gentleman who has once offended her to be restored to her good graces. In all her other connections with family and friends, she must surely exercise both forgiveness and forbearance and readily expects that her nearest and dearest will forgive her in their turn. The willingness to forgive in connections of long duration and firm affection nevertheless depends on an honest acknowledgment of error and a sincere apology for the offense. The husband hunter must expect no less from a gentleman who expects to continue to receive her notice.

—*The Husband Hunter's Guide to London*

Chapter 7

It was near teatime when Nate entered Kirby's. The bell jingled, and the old man looked up from where he sat behind the counter in the gloom of the shop. It was a sign of how low his spirits were that he had yet to fix the broken window at the front of the shop that Nate had boarded up before the club closed.

"Where's Miranda?" he asked.

"In the back. She's very down." Kirby shook his head.

"Let me have a crack at her, sir. I'll bring her out of it."

The old man shrugged, and Nate pushed through the crimson velvet curtains into the passage that led to Kirby's tailoring room, where he had measured the spies—Blackstone, Hazelwood, and Clare—and created for them the clothes each needed to play his role. Kirby had made coats for Nate, too, coats to rival those of the loftiest toffs in London.

He found Miranda sitting on the kilim-padded bench, red-eyed and hunched over a blue silk waistcoat, most likely one of Lord Hazelwood's. She didn't move though she had a sewing case at her side and a needle in hand, a silver thimble on one finger. The glow from a lamp on the table hardly reached her.

Nate steadied himself. For a year he'd made a study of Miranda Kirby, her looks and her moods. He knew just what made her blue eyes flash and her perfect round chin jut proudly. He had memorized the shape of her left ear and the way her white lace tucker moved with her breathing.

Once, he had kissed her, an experience that left his head spinning and his heart aching.

Today her nose was red, and her bright hair looked dull and flat against her skull. She looked up at him and quickly down again. "You," she said. "Go away. I'm busy."

"Don't you want to know why I've come?"

"I won't be mocked."

"I haven't come to mock you." He took a seat opposite her bench, near enough to touch her, but not so close as to crowd her. "I've come to enlist your help."

"My help? Hah, nobody wants *my* help."

"Turns out I do."

"Why?"

"Because a..." He almost said *man*. That was the word he'd used with Captain Clare, but he thought the better of it with Miranda. "...a *spy* needs a partner."

"What spy?"

"Me."

"Oh, you're a spy now?" Her eyes came alive a bit as she challenged him.

"I've got a job to do for Captain Clare. You could come along." He waited while she fretted at the buttons of the waistcoat.

"Where?"

"To a place called Hartwood. It's off the Aylesbury road near High Wycombe. A lord's estate." Miranda's interest always picked up if a toff was involved.

"High Wycombe's near thirty miles away. How do we get there?" She knew he didn't drive, a lack of gentlemanly accomplishment in her view.

"Thirty miles of good road. We'll travel stage."

"And then? We walk up the drive in all our dirt and knock on the door and ask the butler, who is as high and mighty as a lord himself, if we can spy on his lordship?"

Nate wanted to laugh. "We won't be going to the front door. No butler is going to look down on us. We go to the housekeeper."

She appeared to consider the strategy. "What do we say?"

"I've got it figured. Do you want to come?"

She plucked at the silk in her lap with her thimble-covered finger. "You go."

"You want the club to open again, don't you?"

She looked up, and if Nate read her rightly, she looked stricken with guilt. There was something his Miranda was not telling him.

He knew she suffered from more than the closing of the club, for she had developed an unreasonable expectation that the most charming of the spies, Viscount Hazelwood, would marry her. It was Hazelwood's love for another girl, Jane Fawkener, that had brought disaster down on the club. Nate didn't blame Hazelwood. If anyone knew what it meant for a man to be well and truly hooked by a woman, Nate knew, had known from the moment he'd met Miranda with her haughty airs and shop-girl accent, her fiery chestnut curls, blue, blue eyes, and creamy skin. She was like him, caught between two worlds, neither the lady she wished to be, nor a creature of the gutter like the girls of Bread Street.

Unreasonably, he wanted her to come with him.

He'd travel quicker alone, and alone, he'd pass unremarked. Alone, he wouldn't have to worry about enemies they might meet. But he wanted a chance to make her forget unattainable lords and remember that kiss. And he wanted her to see that they worked well together. So he played a little unfairly.

"You're too busy for adventure, I see." He stood up and moved toward the door. "I'll let you put away your needle and get your father's tea on."

She glared up at him. "As if I didn't know my duty." With a few rapid moves she tucked her needle and thimble away in the little case beside her on the bench.

Nate stopped at the door and looked back. "Is it what you want—doing for your father, putting the tea on and tidying the rooms—or do you want to come on an adventure with me?"

She stood up and tossed the bit of blue silk aside. "Oh very well, I'll come with you. When do we leave?"

Whatever her disposition, the husband hunter will want to consider her laugh. It is not necessary that she, herself, be a wit, capable of astonishing a room with clever repartee, but she must be seen to catch and understand the wit of others. It is chiefly through her laugh that she will reveal the liveliness of her mind and spirits. Is her laugh warm and spontaneous? Is it cruel or artificial? Is it dry, hollow, or insincere? There must be nothing of the titter, the squeal, or the cackle in her mirth. If she laughs with delight at the genuinely ridiculous and refrains from laughing at what is small and mean in the conversation of others, her laugh will please whether it sounds like the chirping of birds or the wheezing of an old bellows.

—The Husband Hunter's Guide to London

Chapter 8

When Harry returned to the inn, he found Lucy and Adam on the high-backed bench laughing. The cat stalked back and forth in front of them, her orange-and-white tail twitching in offended feline dignity.

Hearty gusts of mirth shook the old man's torso. Lucy's lighter laughter skipped and danced in bright bursts between soft catches in her breath.

Those throaty breaths hit Harry squarely in the gut. Lucy would laugh in bed, and her breath would come in little gasps of a different sort.

"What's the joke?" he asked. Apparently neither of them felt his nagging sense of danger at a second stage robbery or at Findlater's attempt to remove the old man from the inn. The mitten tucked inside Harry's jacket said they were wrong.

Lucy looked up at him, wiping a hint of dampness from her eyes. "I was telling Adam about the stage passengers, and he said they were like Queenie. I'm afraid she took exception to the comparison."

Harry thought their laughter a bit daft. Lucy's disgruntled stage passengers must have kept her jumping with demands for food and altered travel arrangements, and he marveled that after bearing the brunt of their dissatisfaction, she still laughed.

The cat, evidently regarding Harry as the sensible one of the bunch, rubbed once against his boots and sat down to do some grooming. Lucy looked up. "You have something on your mind?"

"I think you should leave the inn."

"That's plain speaking. Why?" Her expression sobered, and she glanced at Adam. "More threats of imminent marriage proposals?"

"You would not stay if you thought Adam in danger."

"You think he's in danger?" She spoke slowly, a studied calm in her voice. "I do."

She stood abruptly. "More plain speaking. From whom is he in danger?"

"From those who once injured him."

"Why should they hurt Adam now?"

"Your father kept him hidden. Now they know where he is."

"Are you suggesting that I have exposed Adam to danger?"

Harry shook his head. He would not burden her with his suspicions. "You can protect him. Take him away from the inn."

"Take him where?" She crossed to the hearth and heaped a shovelful of coals from the scuttle into the grate.

"I know a place where he can be perfectly concealed."

She stared into the fire. "You take an eager interest in Adam, but we hardly know you. What brought you to us? Why do you stay?"

He studied her profile, both unmistakably female and strong. "Call it kindness from a stranger."

"Kindness?" She turned back to him. "What sort of kindness is it to send Adam away from his home?"

Her frame shook almost imperceptibly. Harry moved to take the coal shovel from her hand, and the cat leapt into Adam's lap, turned in tight circles, and settled between Adam's big hands.

The old man spoke. "You like cats, Captain. You like your ale dark like coffee."

Harry kept his gaze on Lucy. "When you leave the inn, you won't want to leave him behind."

She drew a sharp breath. "When I... Captain, you overstep your authority. Why should I leave my inn?"

"Because you don't wish to wound your neighbors' pride when you refuse to marry any of them."

She let out a short dry laugh, not at all like the merry sound he'd interrupted earlier, but her eyes still danced. "First you presume to know who's going to propose to me, and now you presume to know my answers."

"Leave it to me, and I will have Adam safely away from here tomorrow, while you go to your friends in town."

"I haven't said I will go anywhere." There was an obstinate tilt to her chin.

"But you've been toying with the idea all day."

"What makes you think that?"

"That letter in your pocket. How many times have you read it?"

She pushed down the paper peeking out of her pocket, and he watched as some kind of debate played out behind her eyes. "If I did go to my friends, who would look out for Adam, and how would I know he was safe?"

"I'll send word."

Her gaze was on Adam, her hand on the letter. Harry thought she needed just a little push to persuade her to give in.

A crash of crockery hitting slate broke the moment. The cat jumped down and scurried around the bench. Raised voices erupted from the kitchen.

Lucy's shoulders slumped briefly, but her eyes still laughed. "London, Captain? For me? I think not. Unless you want to do without supper."

A minute later Harry heard her low, calm voice cutting through the girls' squabbling, restoring order.

"The girls need Lucy in the kitchen," Adam said. And Harry knew he had one more thing to do before he could pry the innkeeper from her inn.

* * * *

Lucy did not miss the cat until it was time to ready Adam for bed. The captain's offer to take Adam to a safe place had consumed her thinking through the evening rush and the last-minute calls of the night's guests for tea and warming pans for their beds.

The captain's unexpected offer of help only added to the temptation of Margaret's letter. Lucy could spend a fortnight in society with no harm done. She could have her moment of picnicking on the grass like the lady in the portrait, then she would return to her duties at the Tooth and Nail.

She checked Queenie's dish and found the untouched scraps from the earlier disaster of the dropped fricassee of chicken. When the cat did not come to her summons, she slipped a worn blue pelisse over her shoulders and stepped out into the night with the dish.

The hush of the kitchen garden surrounded her. She breathed in sharp, fresh air, and with one hand, pulled her pelisse tighter. Whatever the calendar said, winter refused to let go of London. Weeks earlier Hyde Park had been the scene of a crazy wager that four horses pulling a huge van could cross the frozen Serpentine.

Now tiny pricks of icy light dotted an indigo sky. As her cheeks and ears cooled, the smell of damp earth rose to meet her. A horse and cart rumbled by beyond the wall, and small creatures skittered under the leafless shrubbery as if passing along a secret roadway in a world apart from the noise and bustle of the inn.

She savored the stillness. In the quiet of the garden, she could acknowledge that though she tried to think of Papa as she worked, somehow the work itself took over. There was little room for thoughts of Papa or anyone else while running to the bells' summons, climbing stairs, lifting trays and buckets, plunging a hand or a mop into cold or hot water, and stirring pots and fires, from first light to last, until every part of one's body ached and reeked of the job. She understood now why Papa had talked so little most evenings. He had been content to let her prattle on about her friends and her school.

She shivered and called Queenie again, lifting her gaze at the sound of the garden gate clicking shut. Out of the dark a man strode up the path. She had a confused impression of his entering. Oddly, he had closed the gate, but not opened it. As he stepped into the beam of light from the kitchen door, she saw black boots, long lean legs, and a scarlet jacket that made a rosy patch in the darkness. Captain Clare.

"What are you doing out here?" he asked.

"Tempting Queenie." She showed him her palm with the dish of scraps. "She's run off."

He waited so long to answer that she thought he must not have understood.

"I didn't think Queenie ever left Adam's side."

"A reproach meant for me, I think, Captain. You think *I* can't leave Adam, but of course, I can and have. Often. For school and Sunday services in town."

"And somehow Adam has survived? Astonishing." He came to stand in the shadows beside her. In spite of the brief joke, his stance was wary and alert, like a soldier on sentry duty. She ventured a glance at his stern profile. She would like to see him laugh once, really laugh, be helpless with it.

He was not like Adam or Papa or the bench sitters, and it was more than the uniform that set him apart. Though he came from the world of her London friends and spoke with their accents, and though Margaret had mentioned him as *charming* in her letter, there was something unyielding about him that said he wasn't entirely at home in London society either, a man who still wore a uniform. Probably, she reasoned, because he was not a man to bend, and certainly not to please a girl. He was about as comfortable as a sheathed sword, and his presence stirred her to vast impatience. "You are quite difficult," she said.

"Am I? Here I thought I was helpful." He continued to look out over the garden.

"You want me to turn my back on my friends."

"I suggested that you go to your friends."

"Not those friends. Adam," she said. "He listens to me and laughs at my jokes, you know."

"I thought that was a husband's job."

She laughed. "Is that what husbands do? I'll have to consult my guide."

"Wise, I'm sure, if you plan to hunt a husband in London."

"I suppose I must, and there's no putting it off."

"Then you'll go tomorrow?"

She laughed. He was that quick to take up the opening she'd left him. "Allow me to make some arrangements, please. And I must find the cat. Either she's gone off mousing, or she's more deeply offended than I thought."

She turned to enter the kitchen, and he caught her by the arm, pulling her into the shadows. Her whole body waited, skin and nerves and breath, for what he might do next.

"I'm not worried about the cat," he said.

He really was a most irksome person. "Is there anyone who can claim your loyalty, Captain? A fellow soldier? A friend? A brother?"

"Or a lover?" he asked, his breath warm against her ear.

She shivered at it. "Oh, pardon me. I should have thought." She turned her face to his.

"There is no lover," he said. This time his breath mingled with hers, his mouth inches from hers, unspoken intention hung in the frosty air. He released her arm, and she hurried into the kitchen.

The husband hunter might imagine that husbands can be found anywhere and that she might spare the expense of a trip to London for the Season. She might consider instead the delights of a fashionable watering hole to which the best of society now and then escapes. Or she might content herself with the gentlemen available in her own circle of four and twenty families. Surely among them are brothers and cousins enough to supply some choice and stir some excitement. Furthermore, she may feel that she can proceed more directly to the altar with a gentleman whose relations are known to her. Here, this writer must speak a word of caution, for such thinking sounds too much like settling, like putting up with inferior accommodations, enduring a smoking chimney, damp sheets, and a lumpy mattress when with a little effort one might have a perfect bed.

—The Husband Hunter's Guide to London

Chapter 9

In the morning it was not Queenie who greeted Lucy from the kitchen, but Mrs. Vell. With a blue pinny covering her usual brown-and-white-checked gown, and her stout, well-muscled forearms bare, Mrs. Vell was rolling out dough on the big pine table in the center of the kitchen.

"Now, miss," she said, applying her rolling pin vigorously to the lump of dough, "I've agreed to forget our differences and keep matters in hand here while you try your luck at finding a husband in London. Mind, you'll want a gentleman that's not too high, nor too low, neither. I'm sure the good captain can steer you right." Mrs. Vell's assistants, Delilah and Sampson, bobbed their heads in agreement.

The good captain? The good captain was going to determine her choice of a husband. Lucy would have a word with him directly. Apparently a red coat gave a man permission to arrange other persons' lives.

As she passed Adam on his bench polishing a tea tray, Frank Blodget assured her he could handle the inn in her absence, and Hannah said, "Captain's in 'is room if ye need 'im, miss."

Lucy marched up the stairs. His door was open, but remembering their last encounter, she halted and knocked.

He looked up from placing folded linens in an open case on the end of the bed, his red coat vivid against the somber colors of the room. The disturbing intimacy of catching him once again in a personal act made Lucy's stomach dip in a queer way. He had told her there was no lover. A lover could watch a man shave or pack or... She wrapped her hand around the doorpost and clung.

"Do you think I can just leave the inn, today?"

He glanced at her, but his hands did not pause in their work. "Yes. A chaise will take us to your friends this afternoon."

Lucy tightened her grip on the doorpost. "You are hurrying me, Captain. I'll go when I'm ready."

He looked briefly at the contents of the case, appeared satisfied with them, and closed it up, his hands quick and sure on the fastenings. He swung the bag to the floor as if it weighed nothing. "Then you'd best be ready at two. Your friends expect you in town for tea."

Lucy let out an exasperated breath. "You seem to have taken everything in hand, but it's my inn." *And my life*, she wanted to add.

His steady gaze met hers. "Take one of the girls to help you pack. Unless you require my assistance."

"Your assistance?" In spite of herself she took a step backward.

"If there's one thing army life teaches, Miss Holbrook, it's packing."

She looked away, fixing her gaze on a long curved sword in a black sheath, lying on the counterpane, its handle glinting in the light. Some senseless, giddy part of her that had no business making decisions welcomed the rush into which he'd thrown her. It was decided. She was going to London. Today. But she wanted the last word in their exchange, a quip or sally of wit that would show him she was seizing the moment, not merely bowing to his will.

He watched her with that unmoved gaze of his that felt anything but cool. No quip came. "And Adam?" she asked.

One eyebrow came up. "Does he have a case?"

"He can have one of Papa's."

"Leave me the key to your father's room, and I'll see to Adam."

She turned on her heel.

"And, Miss Holbrook, be sure to pack your husband hunter's guide."

* * * *

In the end leaving the inn happened so swiftly that Lucy had no time to fix the impression in her mind. With Hannah's help she'd packed so quickly that she hardly knew what was in her two cases. She glanced at her laughing lady as she closed the door to her room. Her lady seemed to urge her to go, and she tried to remember those questions she always asked of her lady. Surely, Papa never meant that in living with her friends in Mayfair she would get above her home. The least forgetfulness of the inn's plain comforts would be fatal to her plan of returning.

When she descended the steps to the waiting coach, the driver was on the box with Adam seated inside. The captain simply offered his hand, lifting her up. Her bottom touched the cushions, the captain sprang in after her, and the horses began to move.

It was the longest seven-mile journey Lucy could remember. The captain took the backward-facing seat, his hands resting on his knees, while she and Adam faced forward. He had that rigid wary posture, his head slightly inclined for listening. In the enclosed space one of his episodes would be harder than ever to handle. Mrs. Vell might consider the captain ruin in a red coat, and as much as his presence unsettled Lucy, she had to admit that he steadied Adam.

Once the coach reached the London road, her old friend fell into a restless state of repetition. She let him know she was by his side with a squeeze of his hand or a word in his ear as he repeated a series of new phrases. She half suspected that Harry Clare had something to do with the new sayings. *Horses very fast. Captain Clare has his sword.* Later—*Adam stays with the captain. Lucy stays with friends.* Each brief speaking spell would end with—*Lucy is the lady now.* The phrases took on the rhythm of the wheels and ran together until Adam fell into a doze.

Lucy wished she could do the same. There was nowhere to look but at Harry Clare's harsh, compelling face and broad shoulders. He could scrutinize her at will, as well, and she suspected he could read her impatience for the journey to end and her London time to begin. If he must judge her, he must.

In Brook Street, the captain's hand in managing her affairs was once again visible. The coach pulled up at the charcoal brick townhouse with its tall windows. Instantly, the door opened, and the butler appeared, directing two liveried footmen to collect Lucy's cases. Captain Clare handed her down to the pavement and offered his arm to help her into the elegant vestibule. Her three friends met her with warm embraces.

"Lucy, dear, you've come." Cordelia sighed.

Margaret gave her a hug and a smile.

"Come, dear," Cassandra invited, "let's warm you up from the journey."

Lucy started forward, then turned back for the door. She made a dash and caught the captain with his hand on the carriage door. "You didn't tell me where you are taking him."

"I'll report to you tomorrow evening. He'll be safe."

She heard Adam from inside the coach. "Lucy is the lady now."

She stood on the pavement, watching as the coach pulled away. It looked as if Adam were leaving her, rather than she leaving him. She realized that that, too, had been part of the captain's plan. The March wind tugged at her hat and cloak, and she quietly vowed not to let London change her.

* * * *

A farmer took Nate and Miranda in his cart down a few miles of country lane from the coaching inn where they'd left the stage. In a thick accent the farmer told Nate how to find the turning to enter the Hartwood grounds. You can't miss it, the farmer assured them. Nate and Miranda had been arguing over the man's words ever since.

Because Miranda had not trusted the inn to keep their belongings, Nate carried their cases. Miranda limped along behind him. She was having a tough time of it, and he was grateful for the sharp wind that whipped her cloak around her and took away half her words.

"Why haven't we reached the turning yet? You must have missed it."

He wanted to say that they'd be there if she had worn sensible half boots instead of fashionable slippers.

"If you have a stone in your shoe," he said, "I can help you take care of it."

"I don't need your help. I need you to find the fogged duck or whatever it is we're supposed to find before night."

Fogged duck was their agreed upon interpretation of the farmer's words. Nate had tried several times to reproduce the man's exact syllables, but he could make no other sense of the sound. He repeated the mystery phrase in his head and kept his gaze trained on the dusty hedge lining the road. It would be cold again tonight, and he hadn't seen anything that looked like a barn. As if Miranda would consent to sleep in a barn.

At the top of a little rise he stopped, waiting for her to catch up. He tried not to look at her. She hadn't told him the real reason she agreed to come with him, but he hoped to get it out of her. As he gazed out over the endless hedge, he saw a tree apparently blasted by lightning at some time in its life. The farmer's *fogged duck* suddenly made sense—*forked oak*. Just beyond the blighted tree a turning opened. Nate gave a whoop of satisfaction and hurried forward, the cases banging against his knees.

"Found it," he called back to Miranda.

In front of him the road sloped down through a little wood to a tree-dotted park in the center of which stood a wide-fronted, three-story house of mellow golden stone. Its rows of tall windows blazed a fiery orange in the light of the late afternoon sun. A stone balustrade crowned its top, and the square tower of a small church rose up behind the building. When Miranda reached his side, she gasped. It was her first view of a grand country house, the sort that looked like an entire street of posh London houses smashed together.

"We're not going in the front door, are we?" she asked in a hushed voice.

"Visitors go round to the housekeeper," he said. Captain Clare had explained the custom and given them the housekeeper's name, and Nate guessed they'd find her in the one-story service wing extending north of the house.

"What if they turn us in for impersonating Mr. Pickersgill's relations?"

"They won't. Come on." They had planned what they would say. As long as Miranda didn't lose her nerve, they'd be fine.

As they came down the long drive, Miranda's limp grew more pronounced, and Nate slowed his pace. No one came out to stop them. When they reached level ground, he led Miranda around to a likely looking door and rang the bell. A pimply girl in a blue pinny and white mobcap answered his ring and stared out at them from a long plain passageway.

"Good afternoon," he said. "We've come to see Mrs. Wellby."

"Well, it's not a public day, ye know," she said. The girl looked warm with work and fires, wispy curls of damp hair curling out from her cap, while Nate was conscious of Miranda standing in the March chill.

"My sister and I have come about a relation of ours," he said.

"A relation, is it?" said the girl. "Yer not the new man?"

"No. We've come to see Mrs. Wellby."

"Avis," said a smooth firm voice of unmistakable authority, "who have we here?"

"Dunno, ma'am. Nobody, I think," the girl said over her shoulder. Having dismissed them, Avis turned on her heel and disappeared through a door off the passageway. A tall woman in deep burgundy silks with a lace collar and a ring of keys at her waist appeared. From her plain calm face and clear bright eyes, Nate guessed she was good at sorting through any kind of nonsense. He began again.

"Good afternoon, Mrs. Wellby?" The woman nodded. "My sister and I have come to inquire about a relation of ours. He may be in service here."

"A relation, you say." She looked them over shrewdly but not unkindly.

"This is Hartwood Manor, is it not?"

"It is, but I suspect you've been misinformed about your relation. Most everyone in service here comes from the village."

"Our relation is quite old now. He may have left service."

"What is his name?"

"Adam Pickersgill."

Mrs. Wellby shook her head. "I'm sorry, I don't know that name." Her gaze took in Miranda's slumping shoulders.

"Please, ma'am," said Miranda. "We've walked ever so far, and we were so sure it was Hartwood where our cousin served."

"You've not been walking our country lanes in those shoes, now have you, miss?"

Miranda nodded. "I wanted to make a good impression when we arrived, you see, but the dust and the wind and..." Her voice trailed off.

"Well, dust and wind we can banish. You'd best come in while we sort out any confusion." She held the door open for them to pass, and directed Nate to leave their cases at the door.

He hid a smile. They'd made it inside. They might still be sleeping rough, but they'd get a hearing and maybe tea. If he got the chance, he'd see to Miranda's feet.

Mrs. Wellby led them along the passage to a wide door. They stepped down into a grand kitchen with stone floors and high ceilings and two large black ranges where pots boiled and roasts turned. A sugar cone as tall as a man's shin stood on the large pine table in the center of the room where three girls, including pimply Avis, worked. Nate's stomach rumbled. He'd choose a warm kitchen, smelling of soup and sugar, over any grand hall in the kingdom.

Mrs. Wellby directed Miranda to a table in an alcove under some high windows. "You, young man, help her with her cloak, and let's get you some tea before you tell me about this relation of yours."

In a few minutes, under Mrs. Wellby's careful eye, a light tea of biscuits and jam appeared before Nate and Miranda. Miranda sipping tea with her ladylike ways made a pretty sight. Nate broke a warm scone in two and reached for the jam spoon.

"Now then," Mrs. Wellby said, watching them, "can you tell me why you need to find this relation?"

Miranda set down her teacup and turned a blushing face to their hostess. "We are orphans. My brother will explain."

Nate cleared his throat. "Until recently our grandfather looked after us, but now he's died, leaving us his money, but naming two guardians over us, his cousin Adam and our uncle Bernard." It was the story they'd worked out in hours of conversation before they ever took the stage. Nate suspected the details came straight from one of Miranda's favorite novels.

Miranda leaned forward as if confiding a deep secret. "Uncle Bernard is a terrible wicked man. He wants to marry me himself to control our money."

Nate took over again. He didn't want their fiction to get in the way of the real job. "So my sister's only hope of escaping a marriage she detests is to find our cousin. Our solicitor told us that Cousin Adam had once been in service at Hartwood."

"That's why we've made this desperate journey to you, ma'am," Miranda added. "Without Cousin Adam we are at the mercy of our wicked uncle."

"Oh dear. Your case does sound desperate. It sounds like something quite out of a novel."

"Oh, ma'am, do you read novels?" Miranda asked.

"I do," Mrs. Wellby admitted.

Nate stared at his tea. That could not be good. Mrs. Wellby might be kind, but he doubted she was a fool. He held his breath. He had yet to take a bite of the biscuit and jam on his plate.

"I just finished *The Marchioness*," Miranda confided.

"Have you?" Mrs. Wellby asked. "Do eat, Mr. Pickersgill, is it?"

Nate nodded. He managed to swallow a bite of biscuit and jam and reached for his tea. He wanted to kick Miranda under the table.

"Have you plans to put up at some inn in the neighborhood until you find this relation of yours? The Three Horseshoes in Sunley perhaps?"

Miranda shot a panicked gaze his way.

"I confess, ma'am," he said, "we've made no arrangements. My sister did not like the look of the coaching inn. It's not what she's used to." He did not say that the inn was far too grand for them.

"Ah," said Mrs. Wellby. She took up her teacup in a slow, meditative way.

Nate swallowed another bite of biscuit. It might be his last for a while unless he could sneak some into a pocket. He hadn't been reduced to such measures in nearly seven years.

Mrs. Wellby lowered her cup again and smiled at Miranda. "I suppose I must help you, as one novel-reader to another. Let's put you up for the night, and in the morning we'll check the record book for your cousin's name."

*As her Season progresses, the husband hunter may wish
to take stock of her prospects. Especially, if she feels she is
meeting the same gentlemen repeatedly without progressing in
an acquaintance with any. She might consider whether she has
overlooked a worthy candidate for her hand. Is it possible that
she should consider the shy gentleman who appears to fade into
the woodwork of a ballroom? Or the man who does not show to
advantage on horseback during excursions to the park? Or the
man who perpetually amuses his dinner partners on the other
side of the tall epergne? To discover a diamond in the rough,
the husband hunter is advised to see whether she can't meet
these gentlemen in a new setting.*

—The Husband Hunter's Guide to London

Chapter 10

The household was up and stirring well before first light. By the time
Nate had dressed and found his way to the kitchen, the room was warm
and bright and once again filled with cooking smells—bread and sugar
and coffee, not the rich dark coffee with the creamy head he'd learned to
make at the old soldier's side, but a passable drink for a cold morning.

He joined Miranda at the table in the alcove and accepted a cup from
pimply Avis. Miranda looked bursting with news.

"How are your feet?" he asked.

She made a little frown. "Fine. Mrs. Wellby gave me sticking plasters
and these little half boots. I dare say I'll do much better today. Do you
know she's read all of Mrs. Raby's books?"

"Show me," he said. Yesterday, he'd imagined sleeping with her in
the hayloft of a barn with their cloaks for blankets and his arms wrapped
around her for warmth.

She swished her skirts aside and stuck out her feet.

"I approve," he said. Tonight, maybe, she would lean against him in the
stage as they made their way back to London.

"You approve! Hah!" she said. "Mrs. Wellby says these little boots once
belonged to the lady of the house, and a very fine lady she is."

He tried the coffee, found it too weak for his taste, and put the cup down. He hoped Miranda had not given them away to the housekeeper. "Listen, Miranda, you must be careful what you say to her."

"I know. I'm not a peahen. Mrs. W offered us a ride back to the village in the estate gig."

There was nothing suspicious in the offer that Nate could see. Probably, Mrs. Wellby just wanted them to be gone. After the first wave of kitchen activity subsided, she came for them. "Now, you two, let us examine the record book for your relation. Follow me."

She led them under the servants' stair through a door into a short dark passageway. At the other end, they stepped into a great hall with a floor of wide polished oak planks and bright with morning light from windows high above them. With the closing of the servant door, they left the good kitchen smells behind. Instead the place smelled of wax and lemons and cold ashes. Mrs. Wellby strode the length of the hall while Nate and Miranda hurried to keep up. At the other end they came out into a smaller hall dominated by a dark staircase, skirted its base, and entered an oak-paneled library with a large desk and tall glass-fronted bookcases. Miranda inched closer to him, so that one side of him was warm, the other cold.

Mrs. Wellby took a key from the ring at her waist, opened one of the cabinets, and turned to Nate. "Now which years should we examine to find your relation?"

Nate swallowed. Miranda touched his sleeve. If anything would make Mrs. Wellby doubt their story, it would be this. "Let's begin with '06, ma'am."

Her brows lifted, but she turned back to the cabinet and pulled a large red volume from the shelf. She laid it open on the desk and flipped through the pages until she reached one with *Lady Day, March 25* written across the top. Leaning over the desk, Nate could see the faint lines that divided the page into four columns. Down the center column a fine sloping hand had written the names of persons serving the household and their positions. To the right a column listed the sum each person had received on that date, the first quarter day of the year.

Mrs. Wellby drew her finger down the page and stopped. "Why, here he is, your relation!" Her voice was full of surprise.

Nate resisted punching a fist in the air. At least one part of their story appeared to be true.

"He was a footman." She kept her finger moving down the page and down the facing page as well. "No one else listed here remains in service today, but Nanny Ragley lives nearby. She might be able to tell you something of that time and your relation."

"May I look, ma'am?" Nate asked.

Miranda shot him a glance for his presumption, but Mrs. Wellby stepped aside. Nate read through the other names on the Lady Day page, the Johns and Thomases and Alberts and the Annas, Sallys, and Pegs who had served the family and their two or three pounds of quarterly wages.

He turned to the page for the next quarter day and carefully read the names again. The list of servants remained the same except shorter. There was no Adam Pickersgill. Nate checked again and found another missing footman, Geoffrey Gibbs. He closed the book. It was curious that two footmen had disappeared from the book between March and June of 1806.

"Well, that's good news, brother," Miranda said. "We know our relation was here."

Nate looked up and found Mrs. Wellby watching him closely. "Twenty years is a long time," she said. "You have no information about any house where Adam might have been employed since then?"

Nate shook his head. "If we may, ma'am, we'd like to speak to Nanny Ragley."

"Of course. I visit her myself once a week with a basket of baked goods from the house. Would you be willing to go in my stead today? Her cottage is not far, and Matthew can take you in the gig."

"Oh yes, thank you, ma'am," Miranda said.

* * * *

Nanny Ragley's one-up/one-down cottage stood along a rutted single-track road next to a copse of beech trees. A low weathered white fence surrounded a small garden. The door lintel sagged under the weight of bare rose canes. A few speckled hens foraged around an oak butt for rainwater, and in the far corner of the yard Nate could see the little shed that housed the necessary screened by a large leafless bush.

Nanny, white-haired and stooped, greeted them at her gate and accepted the basket from Miranda. A green-and-blue-plaid shawl covered her shoulders and crossed over her chest, held in place by a small gold pin.

"She's like the grandmother in the fairy tale," Miranda whispered to him as they followed Nanny into the dark interior of the cottage. A fire burned in the hearth and kept the chill off inside where the sun didn't reach. Nanny set the basket on the table and paused, leaning on her hands, to catch her breath. She waved Nate to a stool by the fire, and Miranda to an old armchair, but Miranda jumped up. "Let me help you, ma'am. I always do, did, for my...grandfather." She cast Nate a speaking glance. He rose and took the old woman's arm to help her to a rustic rush-bottom chair, while Miranda unpacked the basket's contents, a jar of dark preserves, a cheese, and a cloth-wrapped bundle of biscuits.

For a few minutes Miranda moved about the cottage putting the kettle on and setting out three chipped cups under Nanny's direction, remarking how neat and orderly the cottage was.

"Now then, children, you've come to tell me a story, I hear," Nanny said.

Miranda laughed. Nate had never seen her look prettier. He had been right to bring her with him.

"We have," she said and began.

He let her talk, and the tale of their cruel uncle Bernard and missing cousin Adam tumbled out just as they'd invented it. Nate remembered all the times he'd heard Miranda tell gentlemen in the shop her own story of her mother's escape from the drownings in France in spite of the silver buckles on her shoes.

Nanny sipped her tea and ate the smallest bits of biscuit, no more than would keep a mouse alive, as Miranda talked.

"So Adam is your cousin, you say?" Nanny asked.

"Our grandfather's cousin," Miranda corrected. "Did you know him in your time at Hartwood?"

Nanny looked at Nate. "And your grandfather made Adam one of your guardians, you say?"

Nate nodded and set his teacup on the hearth. He recognized skepticism when he heard it.

"I did know him. He was a handsome man with thick dark hair even at his age, and he must have been the oldest man serving at Hartwood. They never raised him higher than footman." Her eyes had the distant look of a person seeing other times and places. "He could put a shine on anything—silver, boots, mirrors."

Nate watched the old woman, waiting for her gaze to return to the present. "Do you know why he left Hartwood, ma'am?"

Nanny nodded and blinked her eyes hard. "I do. He was devoted to Lady Penelope, the old lord's daughter. People said he was her dog. He followed her about and fetched and carried for her. He knew her bell from all the bells in that house."

Nanny shook her head. "The trouble started when she married that Frenchman who disappeared."

Miranda gasped. "A Frenchman!"

"No word of him for months. The old lord wanted Lady Penelope to stay at home until the family could discover what had become of him, but she was mad to go to London herself to find the truth. She thought the government knew." Nanny paused to sip her tea.

Miranda leaned forward in her chair, and Nate gave the old woman credit for being a good storyteller herself.

"She left in the night with Adam and another footman, a cheeky young man. I don't remember his name. She never came back, nor did any of 'em. Never heard a word, never found her, nor the child neither."

"A child?" Miranda's voice squeaked.

"A sweet, sweet girl, all golden curls, still in leading strings. That's when the sorrow fell on Hartwood."

"A child," Miranda repeated. She looked startled by the detail.

"Was that in '06, ma'am?" Nate asked.

Nanny nodded.

"And no one ever found the coach or the coachman?"

"Strange, isn't it. You can imagine what wild thoughts people had. Some suspected Adam was to blame, but the old lord wouldn't hear a word of that. Said Adam was simple, not violent. He'd known Adam as a boy." Nanny shook her head.

Nate braced himself. In telling the story, Nanny Ragley had uncovered all the details that made Nate and Miranda's guardian story less believable. The less he said now the better.

"Odd to name so old a man to be a guardian, ain't it? You don't know where he is, you say?"

Miranda prudently studied her shoes.

Nate met the old woman's sharp gaze. "No, ma'am." It was harder to lie to her than he'd thought it would be. He must be out of practice. Later, if the captain solved the case, maybe they could tell her the truth about Adam.

Nanny's look turned thoughtful. "Don't suppose he's in service again. What will you do next then?"

"Ma'am, you've given us some clues to guide our search. Before, we didn't know where to start or even what Cousin Adam looked like." It was true. Nanny Ragley had given them the beginning of the story. Nate knew the end. He knew where the coach had disappeared and where Adam Pickersgill had ended up. It was the middle of the story they must find. Nate hoped they'd discover the truth riding a Radcliffe Rocket on its night run.

While Miranda tidied up their cups and put the provisions away in Nanny's cupboard, Nate walked the lane to find the gig. When he returned, Nanny and Miranda stood at the gate, arm in arm, the old woman patting

Miranda's hand. Nate shook his head. He was certainly seeing another side of his haughty love. She, who wanted to be a lady, was cowed and quiet in grand spaces and full of talk and laughter in cottages and kitchens and housekeepers' rooms.

He helped her up into the gig and turned to thank Nanny Ragley. The old woman hooked his arm in a strong grip and leaned toward him. "Mind, young man, I don't know what game you two are playing at, but someone's going to see through yer stories, mark my word."

*As the husband hunter consults her post, she naturally
thrills to invitations for balls, routs, and the opera—those
engagements that promise the exhilaration of seeing and
being seen in a glittering crowd among whom are a number
of eligible gentlemen. She holds a ball invitation in her hand,
and her imagination sees eligible partners lining up to claim
her for a quadrille. A word of caution is now in order. In the
pile of invitations, the husband hunter must not disdain the
invitation to a small dinner party. Supposing the guests are only
the hostess's maiden aunt Lady Plume, the easily scandalized
Bishop Pew, a gossip or two, and three married couples without
a single man among them, the wise husband hunter will make
room in her calendar for such a dinner. The small dinner party
is simply the best occasion for the husband hunter to dazzle her
company, and the report, which her fellow guests will willingly
spread of her beauty and spirit, is sure to reach the ears of
those gentlemen who will seek to fill her dance card at the next
ball.*

—The Husband Hunter's Guide to London

Chapter 11

Nanny Ragley's warning came back to worry Nate as he and Miranda
watched the Hartwood gig drive off in front of the Three Horseshoes in
Sunley.

The inn's three stone bays, each with a tall pointed roof, towered over
them. Two mail coaches with their distinctive black bodies and red door
panels passed in the crowded high street, the guards blowing on their yards
of tin, foot travelers scrambling out of the way.

Miranda, who had talked steadily in the gig about Nanny and Mrs.
Wellby, now fell silent and took Nate's arm with unusual docility as they
entered the inn. He managed to haul the two cases into the coffee room
and find Miranda a seat on a bench under the window.

"I'll be a few minutes," he said, more to himself than her. Miranda was
a girl men noticed. Already she was drawing glances from strangers. "To
get our tickets," he told her.

She looked very much the lady in one of those short tight jackets women wore over their bosoms. Little dots on her white skirts matched the blue of her hat and her eyes. There was a quality to her clothes to make ordinary fellows like him hesitate to approach her, but if she spoke in that shop-girl accent of hers, there was no telling what insult she might receive.

From the ticket queue, he glanced over his shoulder, ready to dash to her side if any man accosted her. With his mind on Miranda, he had to ask the agent to repeat. There were no seats to be had on the night run of the Radcliffe Rocket until the next day. Nate paid for two seats for the following night and turned back toward Miranda.

He held the tickets in his hand, half elated, half terrified. They could tell Captain Clare what they'd learned about Adam Pickersgill, and now fate had handed him more time with Miranda, but he had to keep her from unwelcome attention until they got on that stage. For all her shrewdness, she was still an innocent.

He crossed the coffee room and sat down beside her on the bench.

"Well?" she said.

"Listen, they don't have seats for us on the Rocket tonight." He took the tickets and put them away in a safe pocket.

"We take another coach then." She smoothed her skirts over her knees.

"We have to stay the night."

"Here?" She looked aghast.

"No. A smaller inn will be better, but if I'm to protect you—"

"Protect me? From what?"

"Insult. We need a story."

"We have a story. We're looking for our lost cousin."

He shook his head. "We need a story that lets us stay in one room."

"One room! You don't mean it. I can't sleep in a room with you. A lady has her character to think of."

He put a finger to her lips, silencing her. A gentleman across the room watched them over his newspaper. "So I can protect you," he said. "One room"— he made a supreme effort to dismiss the images flashing in his brain—"not one bed."

Miranda's cheeks turned an interesting shade of pink.

"Ready?" he asked.

She nodded.

He wanted to find a less bustling inn, and he wanted to remove her from the too-interested gaze of the man behind the newspaper. Every man's intentions became suspect because he himself had thoughts he didn't want to own about spending the night with Miranda. The best thing was to find decent lodgings and keep them both busy about the town, so that they'd fall fast asleep. But first, they had to get their story straight for a landlord. Landlords, Nate thought, were a far more suspicious lot than housekeepers or nannies.

It proved easier to find an inn than to agree on a story. Off the high street next to a sweet shop was a small brick-and-timbered inn with the modest rates Nate thought prudent. He bought Miranda a bag of peppermints and proposed a simple story. They were to be a Mr. and Mrs. Fulton making a trip to London to visit her mother, who'd taken ill.

"Why are we changing our story?" she wanted to know.

"Because we shouldn't go spreading what we learned to strangers before we report to Captain Clare."

She frowned and sucked harder on her peppermint. "You think anyone in this country town cares about our lost cousin?"

"People know Lady Penelope disappeared. We don't want them thinking we know something we don't."

"Well, we could change the name of our relation and keep the story."

He shook his head. She could be so stubborn. "Do you want to go on sitting in your father's back room, or do you want the club to reopen?"

Her face crumpled, and she looked away from him. He didn't know what he'd said to upset her. The truth was that she didn't want to be his wife even in a fiction. He watched the customers go in and out of the sweet shop while he waited for the sting of it to fade.

After the peppermint had turned to chalk on his tongue, she spoke in a small tight voice. "All right then, I'll do it."

"Good," he said. He hauled her up off their bench and hefted their bags.

Then she spoke again. "But," she said, "you have to wait for me to be in bed, you can't light any lamps, and you have to sleep on the floor."

She was still his Miranda.

* * * *

Cassandra and Cordelia Fawkener's female guests occupied the lilac drawing room after dinner. Lucy had had no word from Harry Clare since they'd parted the afternoon before. Her friends had given her little time to worry about Adam as they helped her prepare for her first London dinner party with a suitable gown and a new way of dressing her hair and a great deal of information about her fellow guests.

Now it fell to Lucy's lot to sit on a pretty velvet settee in conversation with a Miss Sophia Throckmorton, a round-faced girl with enormous dark eyes, an equally impressive bosom, and a gown of such a deep gold it reminded Lucy of Mrs. Vell's best mustard. Miss Throckmorton needed no encouragement to talk. In the quarter hour they'd spent on the settee, Lucy had learned everything she wished to know and more about the girl's aspiration to snare a handsome, titled husband during the coming Season.

"I would not come to a party of such...persons except that our dear hostesses know so very many single men," she confided with a hand on Lucy's. "One must never neglect an opportunity to be seen by those who will praise one's beauty to others."

Lucy was far from certain that Cordelia or Cassandra would praise a girl who looked like a mustard pot, but she held her tongue. She had a suspicion that her friends liked to create a bit of drama at their parties. Nothing else in Lucy's view could quite explain the evening's mix of guests, a fiery MP who had his doubts about the creation of a Metropolitan Police Force, a young baron with radical political leanings, a couple who appeared to be frostily observing a public unity they were far from feeling, and all their dear friends from the Back Bench Lending Library.

The table had been lovely, the food delicious, and the service so attentive as to be nearly invisible, but Lucy had noted an almost gleeful exchange of glances between the two sisters whenever their guests grew heated or the MP thumped the table and made the ivory-handled knives bounce. She had heard Cassandra remark to Cordelia, "If we can't have the Duchess of Richmond's luck, we must make our own."

For a time Lucy had enjoyed watching her fellow guests, but now under the steady barrage of Miss Throckmorton's self-disclosure, she began to feel what a long day it had been and to wish that the captain had not disappointed her. She had been mistaken in trusting both his promise and his apparent interest in her. A womanly mistake her husband hunter's guide said was not uncommon. Now she was as tired as she had ever been after a day on her feet at the inn. She straightened her spine and suppressed a threatening yawn as the drawing room door opened.

Lucy glanced at the door with the happy thought that the gentlemen would join them, the tea tray would soon follow, and bed could not be far behind. But only one gentleman entered the room, Harry Clare, looking startlingly handsome in fashionable black evening wear. He crossed the room to offer his hostesses a brief word and bow, and then, in his direct manner, he came straight to Lucy. She could not look away. Beside her Miss Throckmorton took up an ivory fan and plied it vigorously.

Harry bowed. "Miss Holbrook, I have a message for you from our mutual friend."

"Oh, how is he? How did you leave him?"

"He's very well. He's with an old friend of mine. They have an understanding already."

"Thank you," she said. She felt the weight of the day's worry slip away, and her heart or her vanity, she could not be sure which, whispered that he was interested after all. "Oh," she said. "May I introduce you? Miss Throckmorton, Captain the Honorable Harry Clare."

One brow went up.

"You see," Lucy said, "I've learned something about you today." Cassandra and Cordelia had explained that the captain was the second son of an earl. Without the uniform he seemed a different man from the one who had helped her yesterday.

He bowed again and took Miss Throckmorton's hand briefly.

For a moment no one spoke. With an effort Lucy kept her seat. She wanted to rise and walk apart with the captain in defiance of all that was polite and rational.

"How was your first day in London?" he asked.

"Long," she said.

"Found a husband yet?" he asked.

"Miss Throckmorton and I were just speaking of every young woman's obligation to look for one," she said.

"I'm sure your hostesses will do their best to put you in the way of eligible men."

Miss Throckmorton intervened. "Miss Holbrook is most advantageously situated here with such friends to help her."

Lucy felt the awkwardness of their situation. She wanted to ask much more about Adam, and about him, Harry Clare, without Miss Throckmorton's curious gaze. The door to the drawing room opened again, and the other gentlemen entered. Suddenly, everyone was talking and moving. Harry Clare was going to walk away, caught up in the general air of change in the room.

"You've put aside your uniform, Captain," she ventured.

"I'm not always at war," he said.

Another of the guests came up to him at that moment. Lucy had met her earlier, a woman near sixty. Harry turned and offered her a grin and quick kiss on the cheek. "Aunt Louisa."

"You scapegrace," she said. "You don't get around me so easily. You've been avoiding your aunts for far too long. Now that I've tracked you down, you must tell me about yourself. Out of uniform, at last, I see."

He offered his arm to the older woman. "You've met Miss Holbrook and Miss Throckmorton?"

She nodded. "Come, tell me if what I hear about your brother is true." His aunt linked her arm in his as they walked away.

"Younger son," said Miss Throckmorton.

"What?" asked Lucy. Her conversation with Harry Clare had ended before it had really begun. The vexed question of his interest in her remained.

"He's only a younger son," Miss Throckmorton repeated. "It's terrible when they're handsome like that, but a woman who wants to be secure of a comfortable position really can't be swayed by a man's appearance."

"Of course not," Lucy said.

Miss Throckmorton sighed and gave herself a little shake. "They say his brother, Richard, has ruined the estate entirely."

Lucy now felt she must change her seat or be subjected to Miss Throckmorton's assessment of Harry Clare's finances. With the arrival of the tea tray, she seized her opportunity. "Shall we have some tea?"

A little movement, a few words spoken to other guests, and the business of securing her own cup of tea freed her from Miss Throckmorton. When she dared to look around for her former companion, she spotted her engaged in conversation with Harry Clare and his aunt.

* * * *

Nate clung to a pot of ale in the small taproom as long as he dared. Any longer and the landlord would doubt the story of a young husband accompanying his worried wife to London to care for her ailing mother. Any longer and his imagining of Miranda's preparations for bed would overheat his brain.

He had a bit of experience of women, none of it satisfying. Once in his Bread Street youth he'd admired an older girl named Eliza. He had watched her pass from a brief bold prettiness to coarse misery under the necessity of pleasing hard-fisted men. It was the way of Bread Street. The grand ladies he'd met since that time hardly moved him. They were as aloof and indifferent to men such as he as stars in the sky. Only Miranda combined the plucky cheek of those Bread Street girls before they became women and the haughty elegance of a true lady. She made him witless, and he needed his wits about him to finish the captain's job.

He said goodnight to the landlord, took a candle, and made his way up the stairs to the room at the back of the inn. Earlier when he and Miranda had put their cases on the bench at the foot of the bed, he'd been pleased by the clean and simple comfort of the place. A rag rug covered a large portion of the floor. A painted clothes press and old chest of drawers with a speckled mirror stood against the wall, with a chair and low table near the hearth opposite. The bed looked roomy, and the patchwork counterpane was clean.

In the light of day from two small high windows on either side of the bed the room seemed spacious enough. There was a screen in the corner for privacy.

Only now, as he tried the door, did he recognize how impossible it would be to ignore the presence of another person.

Miranda had locked it as he'd instructed. He knocked. "It's me," he said. "Open the door."

"No lamps," she reminded him.

He waited, listening to her movements. The key turned, the door opened, and he stuck his foot in at once.

"You've got a candle," she cried, smacking the door against his boot.

"Get back in bed. I'll wait."

She let go of the door, and he heard her dash across the room and scramble into bed.

He pushed the door open and turned toward the dresser, keeping his back to the bed. When he set the candle down, his shadowy image filled the speckled mirror. The room smelled of her, of tooth powder, lemon soap, and almond cream. He smelled of ale. He took a steadying breath of air that was full of Miranda.

What he had to do was simple. He'd done it a thousand times. There was no reason that a girl lying in a bed looking at the ceiling should make him feel clumsy and disconnected from his hands. He rehearsed the moves in his mind. *Boots, jacket, neckerchief, waistcoat.* Even when he removed them, he'd still be decently clothed.

"I hung some of your things in the clothes press," she said.

His stomach took a mad dive at the thought of her touching his clothes.

"Thank you," he said. He turned and opened the press, briefly losing his intention in the lavender scent of her gowns. His brain managed to summon the thought—*Boot jack.* He brushed aside her muslin skirts, found the jack, and removed his boots.

"How are your feet?" he asked.

"I've ruined a pair of fine cotton stockings," she said.

"We can look for a shop tomorrow. Did you leave me a pillow on the bench?"

"Yes. And a blanket."

He took a deep breath and shed his jacket, neckcloth, and waistcoat in quick succession, then stood for a moment, his hands full of wool and linen, and his head full of nothing.

"There's a hook in the press for your coat," she said.

He made his hands put away the clothes, then turned to the bench for the pillow and blanket. He tossed the pillow onto the rug and pulled the blanket around his shoulders. Leaning over to blow out the candle, he caught a glimpse of her eyes watching him in the mirror. He blew out the candle. The room went dark, and he stretched out on the cold, hard floor.

Above him the bedclothes made silky sliding noises that unsettled him and left his body on edge. He lay still and waited for his heart to stop racing and his blood to slow in his veins. He wanted to try some deep breaths, but she'd hear him. He had not slept in a room with another person since his days at Bredsell's School.

"What happened to Lady Penelope do you think?" her voice sounded small and lost.

He didn't say what he thought. "If she were in one of your stories, what would happen to her?" he asked.

"Oh," she said, "in a story?" She was silent for a minute. "In a story, she would find her husband and save him from the villains who'd imprisoned him, and she'd smuggle him out of France, and they'd live in a castle in Italy until it was safe to return."

"I like it," he said. He would not quarrel with a happy ending.

"But you don't think it happened that way? Do you think Adam Pickersgill took the child?"

"No." All he'd seen of the old man was kindness and confusion. He doubted Adam Pickersgill had ever hurt a soul.

"You sound very sure. You're always so sure, as if I could never be right."

"I don't know what happened. It's the spies' job to find out, and if we do, the club will open again."

After a moment she asked, "Is it so important to you that the club reopen?"

"It's everything," he said. If she couldn't love him, at least the club would offer work and pay, and a chance to go on rising in the world, far beyond Bread Street.

She didn't answer, but he heard the bedclothes rustling again and the bed frame creaking.

"Is the mattress lumpy?" he asked.

"No," she said in her smallest voice.

Something troubled her, and he waited to see if she would tell him. He should not have mentioned the club. He knew it was a vexed topic. For months Miranda had pinned her hopes and fancies on one of the club's gentleman spies. Lord Hazelwood was a disgraced and disinherited lord who made a charming spy and who would never marry a shop girl. Now Hazelwood had married another.

When he didn't hear her movements any longer, he asked, "Do you still love Hazelwood?"

In the close and empty darkness she made no reply.

* * * *

Harry was out of practice. He had not attended a polite dinner party in years. He had forgotten how admirably some women could maneuver to advantage in the terrain of a drawing room. He knew good tactics when he saw them. Miss Throckmorton was adept at it, while Lucy plainly had no sense of strategy. It was up to him in the last minutes of the evening as the guests moved toward the stairs to get close enough to speak a word in her ear.

"Miss Holbrook, I wonder if you would come for a drive with me in the afternoon tomorrow?"

She looked up with a ready smile and a glow of pleasure in those blue eyes. It was a mystery how a man like Iron Tom Holbrook with his dark hair and brows and a build as square and solid as the Norman tower of St. Botolph's church had come to bear such a fair-haired, blue-eyed daughter. Harry was in danger of getting lost in those eyes.

"You'll want a complete account of how our friend is getting on," he told her, making good on his promise.

Her glance shifted away, her smile dimmed. "Thank you, Captain, that would be kind," she said.

The business of leave-taking separated them again before he understood what he'd said to rob her of that first smile.

As the husband hunter dresses for an outing in London society, she fears that her lack of acquaintance in town dooms her to the sidelines of any gathering or conversation. At times it seems that everyone around her has been on the town forever and that allusions and asides have a meaning to the Londoner that she cannot fathom. At other times London ways seem odd. She is amused at the degree of importance attached to such trivialities as the cut of a gentleman's lapel or the plumes in a lady's hat. She fears that her inexperience and lack of familiarity with London ways will exclude her from good company. But she need not fear. A lively curiosity and an open mind are the only vouchers she needs to be admitted to the best company in London.

—*The Husband Hunter's Guide to London*

Chapter 12

The captain, arriving in Brook Street at the fashionable hour for a drive in the park, met with Cassandra and Cordelia's entire approval for his hat and caped driving coat and the look of his curricle and pair. With a quick survey of Lucy's dove-gray pelisse, gloves, and bonnet, they hurried her out the door to see and be seen.

After he handed her into his carriage, he met her gaze and asked, "What's so amusing?"

"Don't look up," she said. "I'm sure my dear friends are observing us from the window. They're determined to snare me a husband and have given you their seal of approval as the ultimate fashionable accessory for a woman's appearance in the park."

"Accessory?"

"Exactly." She gave him a quick scrutiny and found it was not enough. He was not handsome precisely, but compelling. She wanted to look at him far more than politeness permitted. "Apparently, my being seen in your company will draw the notice of other gentlemen."

"Do you have any in mind?"

"It's early days yet, Captain. Besides yourself and my old friends from our Back Bench Lending Library, I have met few eligible bachelors."

"And you wouldn't bet on a horse without seeing the field, is that it?"

"Exactly, the husband hunter must cast a wide net." Lucy laughed. If he intended to flirt with her, he showed no sign of doing so.

The street was crowded with carriages like theirs headed for the park on an afternoon of warm sun and cool breezes. The trees made a swaying tracery against a bright blue and white sky. The captain handled his pair with ease. It was one more thing about him that drew her attention. When he'd got them through the traffic of Grosvenor Square and the park was in sight down the end of Brook Street, Lucy brought up the true reason for their drive.

"You wanted to tell me about Adam," she said.

"He's with a friend of mine," he said, "a steady man, who keeps a shop with a back room and a small garden, quite concealed from notice. They get on well together."

"Has Adam had any...episodes?"

"None. You've thought about why he has them, haven't you?"

"When I was twelve, I made quite a study of his...frenzies. He had so much distress that summer, and I thought there must be a way to...help him if I could understand what brought on his...fits."

"And did you figure anything out about their cause?" His gaze was on his horses, but he seemed intent on her answer.

"No. Papa made me stop. I wrote down all the things Adam said in those moments. I thought perhaps they made a story."

He nodded, watching her with a narrowed gaze. "And you thought it would help him if you could unravel the story?"

"I did, but Papa convinced me that it would be a selfish experiment to push Adam to relive whatever happened. It might drive him to true madness."

"Would you be willing to risk the experiment now, if you thought it might help him?"

"Perhaps, if I thought him growing worse, or if I truly could not manage to keep him at the inn." It struck her that Harry Clare should have thoughts similar to her own about Adam. She gathered that he had been at war from the long Peninsular campaign through the final decisive battle at Waterloo. He must have been quite young when he began soldiering. She had had a glimpse of his scars, but he had survived. He must have seen other men with worse wounds, perhaps even wounds of the mind such as Adam suffered.

There was a bit of a jam entering the park, and he slowed the horses to a halting walk.

"How do they bear it?" she asked. "They are made for freedom and speed, but we put them in harness and blinders, tug on their poor mouths, and insist that they barely move."

"We ask much more of them than that," he answered.

"In war, you mean?"

"And wherever there's money to be made from their strength. Radcliffe is a notorious abuser of horses, you know."

She shook her head. "Tell me."

"He wears his teams out and shifts the weakest horses to the night run. They die in the traces at an appalling rate."

"So why is someone stealing those horses?"

"I'd like to know."

"Is that why you drove out to the scene of the robbery the other day?"

A brief flash of surprise showed that she'd caught him off guard. "Cole abandoned his passengers. I thought I might offer some help."

It was a quick recovery, but he was not telling her the true reason he'd gone out to the scene of the robbery.

They passed at last into the park proper and joined the fashionable parade. It was plain from the looks and laughter and gaiety of most of the crowd that it was the hour for flirtation. Lucy caught the glances ladies directed at her companion. Perhaps they envied her, but she had to laugh at herself at how little interest in her he showed. Their talk was all of Adam or horses. If she had to sum up his character, she would say that Harry Clare was a man who put duty first, kindness second, and ladies, nowhere. She could put to rest the question of his having any special interest in her. Still, she thought to rally him a little. She was startled from the thought when a gentleman on a tall bay gelding rode straight at them, reining in, blocking their path. Harry pulled the carriage to the side.

The gentleman stared hard at Lucy while he brought his restive mount to order with a harsh application of pressure on the horse's mouth. The lathered animal stood, snorting and quivering.

"I see you've found an heiress already, Harry," the man said.

"Good afternoon, Richard." Harry angled his shoulder forward, so that his body was between Lucy and the stranger. "Miss Holbrook, my brother, Lord Mountjoy."

Over Harry's shoulder Lucy nodded to the earl. His angry pallid face offered no answering acknowledgement. Lucy saw little resemblance between the brothers.

"Time is running out, brother," he said to Harry. "If you're going to marry money, you'd best have the banns called at once and get on with it. I had an offer for Mountjoy today."

"You'll have others, I'm sure," Harry answered.

Richard turned his gaze to Lucy. She met his pointed stare as steadily as she could. "Do you fancy him, girl?" Richard asked Lucy. "Your friends can help you to a better match, I'm sure." He leaned forward in his saddle. "My dear brother has neither charm nor money. I'm surprised he's left off his uniform. It's been his meal ticket for years. I hear he gives a firsthand account of the great battle for a mutton chop and pot of ale."

As abruptly as he'd come, Lord Mountjoy wheeled his horse around and set off down the carriage drive against the traffic.

Harry Clare maneuvered their vehicle back into the moving line of carriages. It was several moments before he spoke. "I'm sorry you had to endure that. I did not expect to meet him here." Nothing in the cool manner of his driving suggested that he was the least disturbed by his brother's anger. "You know Adam talks of you and Queenie. Of the pair of you, he may miss Queenie more."

Lucy swallowed. She understood him. They were to keep the conversation light and teasing. It wouldn't do to say that she thought the unpleasantness of the encounter was nothing for her, a moment's discomfort, while for him the pain of such an estrangement from a brother did not end.

"Queenie, I'd quite forgotten her for the moment. She must have come home by now."

The captain said nothing in reply, apparently preoccupied with his horses in the London traffic.

* * * *

Lucy was becoming an old hand at dinner parties. She tried not to feel the least bit let down at the absence of Harry Clare. He was hardly essential to her pleasure. He had taken her driving in the park. She could not expect him to dance attendance on her.

She paced herself through the inevitable courses and removes on Lady Eliza Fawkener's table, avoided the buttered prawns, kept an overzealous footman from refilling her wine glass, and picked her moment for the ladies' retiring room. But she could not elude her new acquaintance, Miss Sophia Throckmorton.

At the interval between dinner and the tea tray Sophia squealed with delight upon seeing Lucy, and with an unerring instinct for causing discomfort, she settled down to probe in earnest about Lucy's mother.

"I've just learned how dire your situation is! Poor you. You can't be presented at court, can you?" she asked. "Not until you resolve the question of who your mother's people were. I wonder that your father did not make some provision for telling you."

"Oh, not so dire, I think. I can't be presented while still in mourning, in any case," Lucy said.

"Quite so. Your father was innkeeper, was he not? I expect he was just the sort of careful man one expects an innkeeper to be. Did he never mention the church where your parents married?"

Lucy shook her head. She had a sudden rueful realization that as a child she asked more questions about Adam than about her own mother. She had accepted her father's explanation that her mother died in childbirth and that both he and she must not dwell on their loss. "Tell me about your—"

"Oh, well, I suppose you could try St. Botolph's. It is likely that they were married right there, and their names would be in the book. Or..." Sophia bounced in her seat, her splendid bosom covered in old gold braid. "...or, you could try your father's solicitor. Solicitors are shockingly privy to all manner of family secrets, I dare say."

* * * *

Nate did his best to stay awake in the moving coach. Miranda had drifted off miles earlier. Now she leaned against him, her head on his shoulder, one of her hands looped through his arm. The story of her ailing mother and Miranda's beauty had won them the front-facing seat inside. The soft velvet crown of her bonnet rested against his left ear.

They'd survived the awkwardness of waking in their room in the morning, but she'd been in low spirits as they'd wandered Sunley. They had sent an express to Captain Clare to tell him they'd be on the Rocket. Then Nate had dragged Miranda through churches and graveyards, and treated her to linen and lace shops. Only the stockings they'd found to replace her ruined ones cheered her briefly. Still he could not regret their adventure. Wherever they went, he'd turn and catch a glimpse of her profile, or feel the weight of her hand on his arm as they crossed cobbles and climbed stone steps. Now in the rocking coach he enjoyed the warm weight of her body against his and the huff of her breathing. He just needed to outlast his fellow passengers before he looked for anything hidden in the coach's secret pockets.

Nate had noted the coachman Cole as they'd boarded. A smile split his broad red face, and coins from the passengers jingled in the pocket of his many-caped greatcoat. He carried a short tommy, a murderous weapon of weighted whalebone that could extract the last burst of speed from a flagging horse. The Rocket itself was a ton of wood, leather, and steel built for speed by London's premier carriage maker.

Nate did not catch the guard's name, but he didn't like the exchange of glances between Cole and the guard as they entered the coach. Nor had he liked the guard's notice of Miranda. At the moment they bowled along at a steady pace on a road that seemed mostly in good repair. By the dim light of the carriage lamps, he watched the two men opposite him. Once he was sure the other passengers slumbered, he would check the lining of the coach's side panels.

* * * *

Miranda was not sure what woke her. Her bonnet was askew on her head, its ribbons cutting into her throat, and her right arm felt tingly from sleeping on it. An unfamiliar weight pressed her to the seat of the coach. It was Nate Wilde stretched across her lap in a shocking way. He was reaching into a pocket in the side of the coach. She tugged at his shoulder to pull him upright, but he was too heavy to budge.

"What are you doing?" she hissed in his ear. Across from them their fellow passengers snored.

He closed a panel on the side of the coach with a soft click and righted himself next to her. "Sorry, I didn't mean to wake you," he whispered.

"What were you looking for?" she asked, whispering like him.

"There's nothing there," he said, his voice puzzled.

"What did you think—"

Shots, splintering glass, and sudden darkness cut off her question. The horses veered sharply to the left, and the coach leaned alarmingly. Above them the outside passengers shouted. Miranda clutched Nate's arm and held on as the coach wobbled like a blancmange. Just when it seemed likely to topple over, it stopped.

Over the squeaks and creaks of the vehicle and the rattle of harness, a contemptuous voice said, "Cole, you annoy me. What have I said about using a tommy on your horses?"

"They're Radcliffe's cattle, not fit for the clapper most of them." Miranda recognized the coachman's voice.

"Highwaymen," whispered one of the passengers opposite them.

The voice outside spoke again. "Your fellow creatures, Cole."

"Just get on with your business, man, and let me do mine."

Then the highwayman spoke in a foreign tongue. From the woods on either side of the road came a gang of shadowy figures. There were more voices in the strange tongue and the jingle of harness and clop of horses' hooves.

"They're freeing the horses," Nate whispered. "Like the last time." He shook off her hold and turned the latch on the door, pushing it slowly open. That was just like him. She was frozen with fear, and he was going to stick his head into trouble.

Without letting down the steps, he dropped softly to the ground.

Miranda hesitated an instant, then stuck her head out of the door. "The steps," she said to Nate.

He put a finger to his lips and lifted his arms to catch her.

"You there. You're in league with the thieves. Stop!"

She turned to see the guard pointing his pistol at Nate from the rear of the coach. It made no sense.

Then he fired. The flash of it illuminated his face. The shot spun Nate to his left, and he crumpled to the ground in front of her. Miranda jumped. She dropped to her knees in the dirt and rolled Nate onto his back, tearing at his coat, searching for a wound.

Around her she could hear shouts in the strange tongue and moving horses, but her ears were mainly full of the shot. She tore off her gloves and felt his shoulder. Her fingers found the hot blood welling up from the wound. The smell of it terrified her. Nate's blood was leaving him. She pushed down hard with her gloves against the place that bled.

She lifted her head to look for help. A man was leading the coach horses away into the woods. Instinct told her the robbers were about to leave. She would be alone to care for Nate with the man who shot him.

"Wait," she cried to the highwayman.

He turned to look down at her from his black horse. He was nothing like the highwaymen in her stories. His gaze was like ice, like the grave. There was no lace at his throat, no plume in his hat, and not a mark on his horse. The dark brim of his hat hid his features. The moon touched only the black gleam of his pistol.

"Take us with you," she pleaded.

"I beg your pardon, miss. You wish to be kidnapped by a gang of desperate men."

Miranda heard amusement in the toffee voice. Miranda knew her gentlemen's voices. No question this man was a gentleman. "The guard shot my...husband. Please don't leave us with them." She shuddered.

"Curious." The highwayman leaned forward in his saddle. The pistol in his hand never wavered. He turned to the coachman again. "Taken to shooting the passengers, have you, Cole?"

"Go on, man. Ye'll be paid, same as always. We can take care of the rest."

"I think not, Cole. I'll handle this problem myself." The highwayman turned in his saddle and spoke again in the strange tongue. Apparently, he issued orders, for two of his accomplices sprang forward and lifted Nate from the ground.

"Careful," Miranda cried. "He's bleeding!"

"*Cuidado!*" said the highwayman.

A third man pulled Miranda up. "*Señora, ven,*" he said. The highwayman reached down a black-gloved hand, and his companion seized Miranda by the waist, and she found herself hoisted through the air onto the great horse. A strong arm came around her waist.

"Hold on," said that voice in her ear. The horse stood perfectly still under them. Around them the shadowy figures disappeared into the woods. "Cole," the man behind her said, "tell your master our deal is off. Can't have your lot shooting the passengers." The highwayman fired his pistol. The guard gave a yelp and tumbled back from the coach, and the highwayman turned and galloped into the woods.

*To find the true happiness she seeks in marriage, the husband
hunter must distinguish between the attentions of two very
different suitors. Both gentlemen depend on keen observation
for the success of their wooing. The first is the courtier, the man
who has made a study of pleasing his company. He knows how
to flatter delicately and how to please the husband hunter's
tastes and preferences. He knows that she prefers the lemon tart
to the macaroon, the violet to the primrose, a country dance to
a quadrille. The other is the man of action. He never flatters.
He appears indifferent to her preferences. He simply procures
an umbrella in the rain or a chair when he sees her fatigued.
He checks the girth of her saddle and makes sure that she has
an escort to the supper room.*

—The Husband Hunter's Guide to London

Chapter 13

Harry put on his scarlet regimentals and returned to the inn early for
Nate Wilde's report. He had a few moments to himself in the coffee room
over Mrs. Vell's eggs and weak coffee to think about Lucy Holbrook and
her missing cat.

The long-case clock sounded the hour, and the bench sitters arrived, but
not the Rocket. In a few minutes a man brought the news that the Rocket
had been robbed again. The thieves had taken the horses and shot the guard.
Cole had abandoned his passengers. A wagon had been sent for them.

As Harry waited for the inn wagon to bring the stranded passengers, he
listened to heated talk of sending for troops to patrol the woods and break
up the gypsy encampment. He had little doubt that the blame was misplaced.

When the passengers arrived, neither Nate nor Miranda appeared. Harry
could not have mistaken Nate's express. He looked the passengers over for
someone who might give a reliable account of what happened.

Most of the passengers were consumed with their own inconvenience
and united in their abuse of thieves and coachmen alike. Except one fellow
with a military set of whiskers, who, Harry guessed, had more sense than
the rest. He sat drinking his ale and helping himself to rolls and bacon,
without needing to shout or complain. When the surgeon arrived to tend
the wounded guard, Harry sought the quiet man.

"First Royals, were you?" the man asked, looking at Harry's uniform. Harry nodded.

"Jeremiah Frost," the man said, extending a hand. "Formerly of the Thirteenth Light, myself. Do you have any interest in this affair?"

"It concerns a friend of mine," Harry replied. "The innkeeper."

"Well," said the man, "I can't help thinking that this lot has got it all twisted round."

"How do you see it?" Harry asked.

Jeremiah spread the fingers of his left hand, ticking them off with his right thumb. "First, Cole and his guard are in on what happens. Second, Cole directly told the highwayman he'd be paid. Third, the fellow was no ruffian, had a voice like a velvet cushion. Fourth, the rest were speaking Spanish, not some Romany tongue. Don't I know my Spanish from five years on the Peninsula!" Jeremiah paused to take a long draught of ale. "Fifth, they never bothered the passengers for a purse or a watch, but took the worthless horses. And lastly, it was the guard who shot the boy."

"Boy?" Harry asked.

"Young fellow with the whitest teeth, traveling with his pretty wife."

"Where are they?"

"The highwayman and his gang took 'em."

"Took them?" Harry swore. He was used to bad news. Equipment got lost. Foul weather descended. Orders were garbled. One soldiered on. He hadn't wanted a new partner, but Wilde was one he didn't want to lose.

"The wife begged the fellow. She didn't trust the guard at all."

"Frost, thank you. Your account of the robbery is most helpful." It was the guard Harry needed to talk with, preferably now when the fellow was still in pain.

He found the man sitting in Lucy's private dining room. He had been neatly grazed by someone who was obviously a good shot and had suffered more from tumbling backward off his seat. At first he refused to talk with Harry about the robbery, but agreed when Harry suggested that the doctor wait to snap the collarbone into place until a constable could be summoned. When the doctor finished, Harry handed the fellow a pot of ale and encouraged him to talk. This time the fellow had quite a lot to say.

* * * *

Miranda was having a second stay in a grand house, and not in the housekeeper's room either. She had been shown to a blue-and-white lady's room with the most cunning dressing table piled with silver boxes and china scent bottles. Frothy lace draped tall windows.

The strange men who spoke in that foreign tongue had carried Nate into the grand house with its marble entry and sweeping staircases. Then English people, country people with recognizable English faces and voices, had taken over and carried Nate up to this grand room. He'd been stripped to his smalls, so that his wound could be cleaned and dressed. A doctor had come and praised Miranda for holding her gloves to her husband's shoulder. She'd likely saved his life, she was told. Somehow the lie about being his wife stole the pleasure from the praise.

A stout maid with a hardy, unsentimental manner took Miranda away while the surgeon probed for the bullet. The woman found Miranda a gown to wear and a shawl for warmth and promised to try what she could to save Miranda's blood-soaked skirts.

When Miranda returned to the pretty bedroom, pale morning light was coming through the tall windows and the doctor had given Nate a draught of medicine to make him sleep. He lay still and white as death in the grand bed, his beautiful shoulder wrapped in bandages.

His other shoulder, smooth as an ivory brush handle, peeked out from the bedclothes. She remembered when he'd been injured the year before. He'd kissed her then. He wouldn't want to kiss her now. He'd left her alone in their room at the inn, he'd hardly looked at her, and he'd slept on the floor. She had stolen glances at him while he shaved, but he had been cool as ice under her gaze, never looking her way.

It made her think again about why he'd brought her with him. She'd thought he still fancied her, but now she saw that he had been intent on the work for Captain Clare. The whole adventure had been a mission to him. He'd been using her as his cover, so that he could ask his questions about Adam without anyone suspecting he was working for a spy. Well, she wouldn't be foolish over Nate Wilde.

She'd been ever so foolish over Lord Hazelwood. She saw that now, and in her folly, she'd done the really unforgivable thing that caused the club to close. Nate wasn't sweet on her anymore, and he didn't even know what she'd done. If he knew... She shook herself. She wouldn't think about that. She had to help him get back his strength, and she had to figure out how they were to get back to London.

The mysterious highwayman had vanished almost as soon as they entered the grand house. Now that she had time to think about it, she realized that the house belonged to him. For a few minutes in the tall wide entry there had been a flurry of activity, of a butler and liveried footmen, all taking orders from the highwayman. As he strode toward a pair of paneled oak doors, he had tossed his hat and black coat into the hands of a waiting footman. Another footman dashed to push open one of the doors. Miranda saw a book-lined wall.

The highwayman had turned to her. Even in the blaze of lights in the hall, what she saw was darkness. His tousled hair was inky black. His brows and eyes and the shadow of his beard were equally dark. He was as tall and wide as old Goldsworthy, but younger and leaner than the spymaster, not much older than she and Nate.

"You and your husband will be safe here, madam, until we can figure out what's to be done with you."

She did not find the remembered words encouraging, and she reached for Nate's still hand and gave it a squeeze. "Sleep now, Nate Wilde, because I need you to wake up tomorrow ready to act," she whispered.

* * * *

Harry's conversation with the guard had made several things clear. The robberies were a distraction. Everything about them was calculated to summon a figure out of legend—the wooded place, the man in black, the band of supposed gypsies. It was all a bit of theatre designed like a magician's sleight of hand to mislead the authorities. Sir Geoffrey Radcliffe appeared to be the victim of robbers, but the stolen horses were actually no loss.

The guard believed Sir Geoffrey had picked the place for the holdup and paid the highwayman. He was less forthcoming about why he'd shot a passenger, claiming the coach had moved and wobbled his gun hand. And he had no idea who the highwayman was. He spoke of the man in the aggrieved tones of one who felt himself wronged. "Some toff on a lark. Disappears every time with the horses and that lot of rabble speaking their gibberish. He had no call to shoot me."

Harry doubted that the highwayman went far after the robbery. If he really was a gentleman on a lark, he had a place nearby. Radcliffe's weary coach horses would slow any escape, and a man would need a place to conceal them. He would start his search for Nate and Miranda with the country estates bordering the Aylesbury road. But first he would pay Sir Geoffrey Radcliffe a visit.

Sir Geoffrey's place of business in London's bustling Church Street had a prominent sign declaring that the business had been established in 1806 and a ground floor devoted to the carriage trade. The vast lower room housed six carriages of various designs leading up to the famous Rocket.

A sign proclaimed, *Ride a Rocket Today!* The carriages on display stood on platforms, each with a designation of its year and make. Great maps on two walls showed the routes Radcliffe's Rockets traveled. A third wall was devoted with cruel relish to a display of coachman's whips, including the murderous tommy.

A beefy clerk with the battered nose and ears of a former pugilist manned the display room, while another clerk asked Harry his business.

"Tell Sir Geoffrey that I heard that his Aylesbury Rocket is troubled by robberies. I wonder, can he use an armed escort on the night run?"

"You?" said the clerk with the pugilist's battered face.

"Old soldiers find work where we can," Harry said.

"Sir Geoffrey pays a guard," the second clerk said.

"And yet a bold thief continues to steal his horses," Harry replied. "At least tell him I offered."

"Keep an eye on him," advised the first clerk. He turned and disappeared through a door in the wall of whips.

"Mind if I look at a coach or two?" Harry asked.

A grunt was the only reply. Harry took his time walking around the coaches under the hostile gaze of the big fellow. He studied the maps on the wall. Each of the Rockets' several lines converged on Dover, and Harry realized he had seen Radcliffe's routes before on a map in Goldsworthy's office at the club.

A canvas-draped vehicle at the rear of the room caught his eye. Its size and shape and the wheels visible below the canvas drape suggested a private rather than a commercial vehicle.

"You've got a coach that's not on display." Harry took a step in the direction of the shrouded carriage, and his path was immediately blocked by the substantial personage of the pugilist clerk.

"That 'un's not restored."

The second clerk returned. "Sir Geoffrey says to leave your name."

"Captain Harry Clare." Neither man wrote the name down.

Across the street Harry waited behind a beer wagon. As he expected, Sir Geoffrey's clerk emerged from the office and summoned a hack. Harry followed the man to a fashionable address on Curzon Street, an address Harry knew well, the lodging of a Frenchman with long ties to the Foreign Office. Goldsworthy had explaining to do, and Harry had friends to recover, but first, he had a picnic to attend.

*As she begins her Season, the husband hunter may feel
that her matrimonial aim is so well known to those around
her when she arrives in London that she can do nothing to
achieve it. She may imagine that every rival miss, every eligible
bachelor, and every sharp-eyed mother of marriageable sons or
daughters has anticipated her intention and her tactics and is
working to achieve a contrary aim. But if our husband hunter
will consider the behavior of true opponents meeting in battle,
even opponents as well acquainted with each other's tactics as
rival generals who have met in the field before and studied the
ground well, she sees at once how fatal it would be to assume
that her rival's victory is inevitable.*

—*The Husband Hunter's Guide to London*

Chapter 14

The day's weather favored a picnic. Cassandra and Cordelia had decided that in spite of the apparent gaiety of such an outing, a picnic was more proper to a true state of mourning than endless rounds of calls on slight acquaintances. In their opinion the tranquility and simplicity of the natural scene, the buds and shoots of spring, and the opportunity for quiet reflection away from the noise and confusion of London would certainly do Lucy's spirits good.

Accordingly a gown in a shade of gray the sisters called "cloud" with black ribbons for her bonnet was to be Lucy's outfit, and the high open ground of Parliament Hill in Hampstead four miles away was to be their destination. A flurry of messages from the Brook Street house brought round nine people for the affair. A pair of barouche-landaus set off by noon with the five ladies, a pair of footmen, and a handcart with a hamper, a basket of drinks, and blankets. Four gentlemen on horseback accompanied the ladies. Lucy tried hard not to be disappointed that Harry Clare was not among the men. The inescapable Miss Throckmorton and her mother were of the party. Miss Throckmorton wore a day dress and matching spencer and bonnet, in a yellow that any dairymaid would be proud to see emerge from the churn.

In their carriage Miss Throckmorton began at once the subject of mothers. "I appreciate how fortunate I am in my mother now that I'm out.

In the schoolroom one hardly realizes the advantage or disadvantage one's parent may prove to be in society."

Lucy murmured that it must indeed be a comfort to have a mother's guidance for the Season.

"What have you discovered about your mother since we last met?"

Lucy conceded that she had no new information to offer.

Miss Throckmorton looked grave. "Well you must pursue it, you know."

Lucy nodded. "I intend to."

"Now, my mother, even at her age, with her appearance and figure, and of course, with her lineage, is the perfect chaperone. It would be dreadful to have a mother who looked a fright. Gentlemen might suppose that one was headed down that path oneself."

For a few blessed minutes this stream of self-congratulation was interrupted by Cordelia bringing up the history of Hampstead, the benefits of its waters, and the many famous personages who resided there.

Lucy managed to avoid further discussion of mothers during the remainder of the drive. The carriages halted at the entrance to the heath, and they descended to climb a rutted wagon track through faded grasses, picking their way between hard frosted ground and softer, boggy patches with Cassandra exhorting them to mind where they stepped, and the footmen stoically pulling the handcart. Lucy thought she would chide her lady about those laboring footmen when she returned to the inn.

The view from the top of the hill was worth the effort. The ladies held their fluttering hats in the breeze, while Lucy's friend Thomas Bickford, the barrister in their Back Bench Lending Library group, pointed out the distant dome of St. Paul's and the spires and roofs of other famous London edifices.

A thick rug was spread on a relatively dry patch of ground, and they sat to enjoy sandwiches, cakes, and hothouse strawberries. *Is this what you wanted for me, Papa?* The question popped into Lucy's head unbidden, and for a moment she could not taste her sandwich. Miss Throckmorton began to speak, but Cordelia cut her off, bringing the conversation round to books. Lucy smiled to herself as the Back Bench group dove into their usual talk about the latest novels they'd read. They were a comfortable group.

An hour passed swiftly by. Miss Throckmorton put aside her plate of strawberries and declared that she would like to explore the woods for primroses and violets. The younger members of the party set off at once while the sisters and Miss Throckmorton's mother dozed in the afternoon sun.

Though there was little foliage, the wood was shady and cool. Miss Throckmorton led the way, skipping happily in the lead. Lucy lagged behind, and when the group surged forward in pursuit of a promising clump of green shoots, she simply stepped off the path, skirted a huge hollow tree, and wandered off. The wood smelled of damp earth and sweet air. The voices behind her faded, and she heard only the flutterings and rustlings of unseen birds, the chattering of a jay, and above her the branches stirring in the wind.

She had no idea how far she wandered before she stopped beside another hollow tree and climbed the arch of its gnarled roots to look out over the wood. There was nothing in bare branches and piles of leaves to make her think of Harry Clare, and yet her thoughts turned to him. She seemed as attuned to his absence as his presence. She had been around plain, honest working men. He was nothing like them. She had thought it was his soldier's jacket that made him appear to be other than the men she knew, but in London, where he no longer wore the scarlet jacket, she saw that his coat didn't matter. He was war-marked even without the coat.

She had thought Papa overly proud to have a genuine Waterloo hero staying at the inn. She had thought little as a girl of England's distant army. She'd been a child, not even at Mrs. Thwayte's, while he'd been at war. Other men had gone about their business getting and spending, while he'd been at war. He'd been little older than she was now on the day of the great battle. She thought he had not yet let go of that day.

A bird took noisy startled flight somewhere behind her. She understood why she'd wandered so far. It was to think of him. Now it was time to turn back. She did not wish to alarm Cordelia and Cassandra. And Miss Throckmorton was right that Lucy should write directly to her father's solicitor. She would send a letter in the morning. She laughed at herself. Men would be amused at the amount of time ladies devoted to thinking about them while they thought only of their own pursuits and not of ladies, at all.

With that resolution she looked around to get her bearings and found she was no longer alone. Harry Clare stood not four feet away watching her with an amused gaze.

"How did you find me?"

"You laughed. Did you want to share the joke?"

She shook her head.

"And," he said, coming to stand at the foot of her tree, looking up at her, "you left a trail the whole army could follow through the dead leaves. Your shoes must be ruined."

His standing so near changed the landscape of the wood. A minute earlier it had seemed an empty place; now it pulsed with life. She looked down at her muddied shoes and damp hem. Leaves clung to her skirts. "Oh dear, I'll be in disgrace."

"Not with your friends. They'll be relieved to have you returned to them." He looked around. "Not a place to hunt a husband, is it?"

She shook her head. Hadn't she conjured him by thinking? "It's an enchanted wood where anything can happen."

"You should be tenderly flirting with four gentlemen at once."

"Should I?"

"Confess. You let Miss Throckmorton drive you from the field?"

"I did," she laughed. "She makes husband hunting seem quite effortful."

His gaze altered. He looked at her in that way he had that heated the blood in her veins. He was not a comfortable gentleman like her Back Bench Lending Library friends. Around those gentlemen she was quite at ease, while around Harry Clare she was impatient, on edge.

"There's no comparison," he said. "Any man with eyes and a bit of sense will choose you."

"How do you know that?"

For answer he reached up a hand to bring her down from her perch.

It was a fine strong hand, and the thought of that hand touching her and undressing her sent a rush of heat through her. "I am not asleep now. I will know if you touch me."

"I hope so," he said in a low husky voice.

She took his hand and felt the contact everywhere at once. Her body tilted toward him, and with a rush of little steps she descended. He steadied her as her feet touched the ground, and kept hold of her hand, but stopped short of drawing her closer.

His smile faded. "You've just begun to hunt a husband. Give it time."

She looked at him, so near, but holding her at a distance when an instant earlier it seemed she must fall into his arms. "Must I? What if I want the husband of my heart to appear at once?"

"Maybe the fellow needs time. He might see you and want you, but he might need to put his own affairs in order before he can ask for your hand. He might not be as prosperous a fellow as a blacksmith or a water flask dealer. But never doubt he would choose you."

He was being kind again.

A shout from one of the picnickers made them both turn. There were Mr. Bickford and Miss Throckmorton.

Harry Clare dropped her hand and offered his arm instead to lead her back. Miss Throckmorton talked about primroses as they made their way through the woods. Cassandra and Cordelia exclaimed over her and their worry, but did not scold.

Harry Clare came to her side again as she climbed into the carriage and contrived a few private words.

"I must leave London for a few days," he told her, leaning against the carriage door.

"What? You would abandon me to the Miss Throckmortons of the world?" she whispered, making a joke of his leaving.

He glanced to where Miss Throckmorton and her bosom had captivated a pair of gentlemen in the party. "Afraid she'll take all the gentlemen for herself?"

"I'm sure she'll throw one or two back into the pond. When do you return?"

"I don't know how long this business will take." His expression was closed, as if some thought or worry related to his journey preoccupied him. He did not say what that business was, but she guessed at the urgency he felt.

"There's a musical evening later this week." Lucy waited for him to say that he'd attend, but he only quirked a brow.

"A musical evening? Is that a happy hunting ground for the husband seeker?"

"So I'm told."

Lucy was growing used to such conversations with him. It was not hard to explain his refusal to kiss her. He might flirt a little, a very little, but he knew the obscurity of her origins. He was an earl's son and the only unmarried man she knew in London who had seen her in a sauce-stained pinny scraping a pike off the floor. The other gentlemen she met knew her as a woman of property acquainted with such visible friends as their hostess.

"I don't want you to think me remiss in any duty to you. Your friends will keep you amused and allow you to cast that net of yours wide in my absence."

She nodded. He was bringing their conversation to a close, and she cast about for a way to keep him talking a few minutes more. "I'm sure you never shirk a duty, Captain. When do you leave?"

"At a most unfashionable hour for a lady, I assure you. Only delivery vans, cattle herds, and night soil wagons will be stirring."

Lucy wanted to protest that she was an early riser. At least, as an innkeeper she had been, but London ways were taking hold of her. "Then I'll not see you off," she said lightly. "London ladies must sleep through the freshness of the morning if they are to dine and talk for hours by candlelight."

At least she made him laugh, and he had not yet turned away, though the horses tossed their heads, eager to begin.

"Do you pass the inn on this journey of yours?" she asked.

"I do," he said.

"Would you ask whether Queenie has returned?"

He looked away for an instant, as if he found her request awkward.

"Of course, as long as you don't require me to smuggle the cat into the Fawkener household."

"Would you? Queenie's just lady enough for London."

"I'll be at your service when I return. And you may be sure that Adam will remain safe."

The husband hunter may imagine that a gentleman with an inclination to favor her as the source of his future happiness needs steady and extensive doses of her company in order to fix his resolve. In truth a little absence may do the trick. The man who finds himself fasting from the sweetness of her smiles and her particular laugh returns to the table starved for what he has missed.

—*The Husband Hunter's Guide to London*

Chapter 15

Harry gave the elusive highwayman credit for covering his tracks well. It took three days of scouting to find the well-concealed pasture where Radcliffe's stolen horses grazed. A few more inquiries led him to the owner of the pasture, Sir Ajax Lynley, Baronet. The gatekeeper at the lodge directed him up an elm-lined avenue to a stone house with jutting bays of windows, pointed turrets, and strolling peacocks. The place was called Lyndale Abbey.

The butler seemed to expect him and led him into an old-fashioned room, its walls hung with red damask and paintings with distinctly religious overtones. Robed figures with marble-like faces made their way through dark landscapes. Harry guessed them to be saints by the halos glowing above their heads. He did not at first see anyone in the room. Then a figure lying on a long couch came to life and rose to his feet. With his height and size the fellow would make a menacing highwayman.

This morning Ajax Lynley wore the buckskin breeches, boots, and buff coat of a country squire, but his dark looks and powerful shoulders suggested a man who would find country life tame. He was younger than Harry by perhaps five years, and his idleness did not conceal a pent-up energy. He might be a man to hold up a Rocket if for no other reason than to escape the sameness of his existence and the disapproval of the saintly figures looking down on him.

Whatever his reason for holding up the Rocket, Harry could only regard the taking of the horses as a rescue rather than a theft. He hoped the abduction would prove to be the same.

Lynley studied Harry. "How may I help you?"

"You could assist me in my search for two young friends of mine."

"Search?"

"They went missing from the Radcliffe Rocket a few nights ago. He may have been shot. I want to be sure they receive shelter and a doctor's care."

"Ah," said his host. "Refreshment?"

"Ale, if you have it," Harry said.

Lynley rang and gestured Harry to a seat. Harry took a chair where he could look out the tall windows at the wandering peacocks on the lawn.

"And you think I can help you with your search?" Lynley asked.

"Situated as you are not far from the Aylesbury road, you may hear something," Harry suggested.

A footman brought a jug and two ale cups.

"Who are these two, it is two? That you are looking for? Relations of yours?" his host asked, pouring from the jug.

Harry recognized a cool-headed opponent. He had no idea what story Miranda and Nate had told their captor, but he could not claim that they were family. "They are unmistakable, I think. She's quite a beauty, and he's got ears and a set of white teeth that must draw the notice of anyone who sees him. They were to meet me at the Tooth and Nail at the end of their journey."

There was a slight pause in Lynley's ale pouring. "You're not still in the army, are you, Captain?" He handed Harry a cup and returned to his lounging.

"Old army habits persist. One doesn't like to leave comrades behind on a mission."

The giant's brows shot up. "An intrigue, Captain?"

Harry tried the ale. "An old soldier from the Thirteenth Light happened to be a passenger with my friends on the Rocket the other night. His account of the incident leads me to believe that they were in more danger from Radcliffe's guard and coachman than from the highwayman who held up the coach."

"Troubling, I imagine," said Lynley.

"It is." Harry set down his ale. "The third holdup of the Rocket in as many weeks, the second shooting of a guard. Talk of a gypsy gang operating."

"There is a habit of blaming the Romany, but I know of no gang in the neighborhood. The magistrates would act swiftly if there were."

"So, I must continue my search," said Harry.

"Are the authorities no help to you?" Lynley asked.

"Have they come to you?" Harry asked in return.

Lynley shook his head.

Harry stood. "They will, but in the meantime if you hear of my friends, or can help them return to the Tooth and Nail in St. Botolph's, I'd be grateful," Harry said.

"You should not worry so much, Captain," Lynley said. "Most likely someone in the neighborhood has offered shelter and a sawbone's attentions to your lost friends, and they will get word to you as soon as they are able to travel."

Lynley's cool face gave nothing away, but Harry understood. The cordial baronet saw Harry to his horse.

* * * *

Nate did not know how long he'd been in the soft lavender bed, but he knew he needed to get out of it. A few times he'd wakened to look at the ceiling like a frosted cake and doze again. Or he'd wakened to Miranda's urging that he swallow some broth. He was useless. He hadn't got them free of the giant or back to Captain Clare.

He opened his eyes to find Miranda with her face pressed to his free hand, weeping.

"What's wrong?" he asked.

She lifted her head. "You're awake."

He nodded and tried to push himself up. He really needed to get out of the bed.

"How's your shoulder?" With the back of her hand she wiped the moisture away from her eyes.

"Aches some," he said. Not his most pressing concern. "Can you help me get up?"

"You can't get up." She jumped to her feet.

"I have to," he said. He pulled the bedclothes away from his legs.

"Oh," she said with a sudden blush of understanding. "I'll help you. There's...what you need in the dressing room."

He slid from the bed, and she offered him a hand, steadying him as he landed on his feet. She lifted his hand around her shoulder and put an arm around his waist, and they crossed a carpet softer than many beds Nate had slept in. At the dressing room he grabbed the doorframe. "I can manage from here."

When he reemerged from the dressing room, he felt his nakedness. He was in smalls and bandage with a good bit of beard on his face and film on his teeth. If he meant to impress Miranda with his gentlemanly appearance, he was failing miserably. She was staring at him. He must cut a miserable figure up against the gentleman highwayman. He was also probably breaking some rule of conduct that said gentlemen didn't appear naked before their wives.

"Do we have our cases?" he asked.

Miranda shook her head. "But the people here have been kind enough to give me things. See, I've got my gown back without the stain."

"Do you have tooth powder?" His mouth had the most disagreeable taste of broth and medicine.

"I do, but you can't mean to use *my* toothbrush?"

He raised his brows. That was probably a rule, too, but he was beyond the rules now.

"Oh, I'll show you." She brushed by him, smelling sweet and fresh as she always did. She was probably enjoying her stay in a grand country house with a handsome highwayman for a host.

She showed him the cabinet with the water and basin and handed him her brush and tooth powder. "Their powder is not as good as Papa's. I told them they should patronize Kirby's in London if they wanted superior powders and soaps."

"Do you know where my clothes are?"

She nodded. "What are you thinking?"

"We have to get to Captain Clare. How long did it take to get here?"

She turned away while he brushed his teeth. "I don't know. It seemed like a very long time, but it could not have been, could it? It was still night when we arrived, and close on morning when the doctor finished with your shoulder."

"Not more than a two hours' ride, then?" he said, finishing up with the towel. His mouth felt much better. He would deal with the beard later. He knew there were footmen who came and went. He would ask one of them about shaving.

"Less, I think," she said. "What do you think the highwayman means to do with us?" she asked.

"We're a problem for him because we've seen his face. We know he robbed the Rocket, but we also know he's a gentleman. He won't want us talking to the authorities."

"We don't have to, do we? We could tell him we'll never speak of the incident and thank him for his kindness to us both."

His kindness to her. Nate shook his head. "Constables will want to talk to us."

"We could tell them he didn't really rob the Rocket. He took the horses, but he didn't take any of the passengers' watches or purses or anything."

"It's the truth," he said. "And we don't know his name or where we are, but we are going to leave."

"We can't just walk away."

"We have to. Tonight."

The musicale or private concert is an event that may both delight and test the husband hunter. Of course, she must attend. As England's enduring poet says, "Music is the food of love," and only in London will the husband hunter hear performers of rare talent and training capable of the full range of musical expression. So universal is the appeal of music that everyone of the first rank will be there. Such an evening places demands on the husband hunter's attention, her taste, and her endurance. There is no more grievous offense at such an event than falling asleep to the pure intonations of a renowned soprano.

—The Husband Hunter's Guide to London

Chapter 16

Lucy thought it not least among the delights of the musical evening at the Marquis of Hertford's house that she could easily lose herself among the five hundred or more guests and one Italian opera company. Miss Throckmorton would never find her in such a crush.

She gladly followed Cordelia and Cassandra to a small salon where a mere hundred guests gathered to hear the new musical director of the English Opera House. He had composed an opera in English, soon to be performed featuring the soprano, Miss Cawse, a great favorite of Lucy's friends. As they hurried forward, and as other guests made way for them in their distinctive matching gowns, Lucy slipped to the back of the crowd. She found a convenient marble column against which to stand. The nearby door of a small antechamber admitted a slight, refreshing stir of night air.

For three days Harry Clare had been absent from London, or at least from those gatherings where Lucy was to cast her net for a husband. She had a chance to consult her little book. It made her laugh. It revealed much of the society around her, but it did not explain the perplexing behavior of her own heart. She had now received compliments from a handsome young baron, a brilliant inventor, and several dashing, if untitled, gentlemen. It remained a puzzle how a man who had, at best, a few words for her at the end of an evening, always words about her absent friend or her missing cat, framed as a military field report, could be so necessary to her pleasure at an evening's entertainment. Only once when he'd found her in the woods had she thought him interested her. The intensity in his gaze said he wanted what she wanted.

* * * *

She had said the event was a musicale. Harry thought it more like one of the mass gatherings of protestors the army had been called upon to quell at the end of the war. And he would have spent hours searching for her except for the Fawkener sisters' habit of dressing so completely alike that every footman had noted their passing from the grand salon of the house into a smaller room with a less famous musician. It helped that Harry knew the house. He'd once courted a girl here.

He'd changed since then. The army had been good for him even if he had had to give up being the boy he had been. He had liked the army, but hated that he was expected as an officer to despise his men, to regard them as the scum of the earth. He could not disrespect a man willing at a given moment to face fire and give his life for another man. Nor could he despise the man who kept his gear and himself in order, willing to march twenty miles in a day and fight the next. Finally, he had been unable to lead British troops against British subjects on British soil, so he'd left the army.

Lucy Holbrook now wore the disguise contrived by her friends for battle of a different sort with the Miss Throckmortons of the world. When he'd first seen her standing on the gnarled root ball of a hollow tree, he had thought her altered beyond recognition. His practical princess had changed her wool dress and pinny for an elegant silk gown for a picnic in the woods. She had spoken of his touch, and he'd thought at once of what lay under those silks. The sisters must have supplied her with a lady's maid, who could lace her stays. The sensible front-closing corset would lie in a drawer until her return to the inn, if she did return. But when she spoke, she was the innkeeper's daughter, the woman who patiently held an old man's hand, fed a cat, and didn't hesitate to do the work she asked of others. The relief of it had been profound.

Three days without a glimpse of her had been quite enough. The delay with the case frustrated him. He had resisted Lucy Holbrook as long as duty required, but he did not think he could resist any longer. He had shed one uniform. He was ready to shed another.

He didn't know what to tell her about the missing cat.

* * * *

The column at Lucy's back was exquisite, and the music was sublime, by turns lilting and soaring, but she was in danger of succumbing to the heat of the room and the length of the composition. She raised a hand to cover her mouth, when her wrist was seized in a firm grip, and she was drawn behind the column through the anteroom door and brought face-to-face with Harry Clare. She put out her free hand to check her momentum and pressed against wool and silk and male.

"Hello," he said, teasing lights in his eyes. "Waiting for someone?"

"I was engrossed in the music," she said. She was firmly on her feet now and should withdraw her hand, but the hard strength of him was so satisfying to the touch.

He laughed. "Confess. I caught you in a yawn."

"Only because of the heat of the room and the lateness of the hour. You know I am not yet accustomed to London ways."

One brow rose. "Aren't you? You know how to avoid your chaperones to have a private moment with a gentleman."

"Unfair. You pulled me away when I was simply trying to catch what little movement of air there is in such crowded rooms." She curled her fingers closed and let her hand fall away from his chest.

"Is it air you want?"

"Yes."

"Sure?"

"Air," she said firmly.

"Come with me, then." He tucked her arm in his and led her out of the anteroom into a long shadowy corridor. At its end they took a flight of steps and then another until Lucy was breathless. He paused only to open a door that looked to be a closet, but which concealed a narrow unlit wooden stairway.

"Hold on," he advised.

There was no chance that she was letting go. They went more slowly until he opened a door and cool night air met them. He helped her out onto the roof of the grand mansion. The lights of Mayfair glimmered in the darkness below, the soft circles of carriage lamps, the flare of torches to light the mansion steps, and candles in windows across the square.

"You know your way around this place." She leaned against the parapet and shivered at the contact with cold stone, and he shed his coat and wrapped it around her shoulders.

He leaned next to her. "I was here once before. I came home from the Peninsula after Fuentes de Oroño to recover from a wound."

"And brought a young lady to the rooftop?"

"I did," he admitted.

"And did she like the view?"

"Yes, but not the idea of marrying me."

"You made an offer of marriage to a lady on this rooftop?"

"She refused me."

She turned to look at him, unsure from his tone how he felt about the revelation. His profile looked as unmoved as ever. "Because you are a younger son."

"That explanation might soothe my pride, but I think she didn't love me."

Lucy wanted to argue that it couldn't be true. "You were young?" she said.

"Nineteen."

"Perhaps you did not cast a wide enough net for a wife."

"And I had no wife hunter's book to guide me. What does your book say about going to a rooftop with a gentleman alone?"

"Oh, my book says, don't do it! My book says I may offer only the warmth of my gaze and the pressure of my hand as signs of favor to any gentleman to whom I am not betrothed."

"And should such a gentleman, not being a reader of the book himself, importune you for further signs of your favor?"

"Would such a gentleman make impertinent advances to an innkeeper's daughter?"

"Oh yes. He might take her hand..." He took Lucy's hand as he spoke. "And draw her close to him, gauging her resistance each step of the way."

Lucy held her breath, offering no resistance as he fitted her body against his, joining them from breast to hip.

"And he'd keep his gaze fixed on her mouth, looking for her to turn that mouth up to him with parted lips."

"Oh." The syllable escaped her, caught in the act of opening to him, and for an instant she leaned back. Then she laughed and shook her head and lifted her face to his again. And he kissed her.

And it was the thing she'd been wanting without knowing that she wanted it, without knowing what it would be, discovering as it went on how right it felt to be held in just this way, and how by answering the pressure of his mouth with hers she could speak to him from her heart as freely and frankly as she had ever spoken to anyone.

His arms tightened around her. The kiss extended from their mouths to every place where their bodies strained against each other. She wrapped her arms around his ribs, holding on, feeling the play of muscle in his back.

A part of her brain tried to catalogue everything she needed to remember about the moment, the cat's tongue roughness along his jaw, the deeper note in his voice, the way his hands cupped her head, his fingers pushing into her hair, his thumbs against her cheeks, and the longing of his person for hers.

The joy of it made her dizzy. A kiss was such a small distance closed. A yielding of but a few steps would go unnoticed on the battlefield in the surge of combat, but between lovers meant the end of resistance, the laying down of arms in a shared victory.

The rattle of carriage wheels and a burst of laughter below them woke Lucy from the dream.

He broke the kiss, slackening his hold, stepping back, his hands slipping away from her waist. He worked to command his breathing. He became himself again, the soldier, saying in a light tone, "That's probably enough impertinence for one evening. I will return you to your friends."

No. She wanted to protest. She had received no training at Mrs. Thwayte's School in how to stop a kiss. All that she'd learned there about giving up her seat near the fire and never taking the last biscuit from the tray had not prepared her for the consuming desire she felt. One did not ache for a seat by the fire or a biscuit.

Sense intruded. They were in London. She was in the care of her friends. She swallowed and nodded. He extended his arm, and she took it, letting him lead her on shaky legs back to the stairs.

They could hear wild clapping as they retraced their steps to the salon. He stopped her at the door of the anteroom, giving her a quick scrutiny, as if her unaltered outward appearance could restore them to mere acquaintance.

She stood her ground and lifted a brow.

Then his face changed. A laugh that made him seem young and foolish, but wiser for such foolishness, shook him and lightened his expression, chased away the furrows on his brow. "You've won, you know. Duty is no match for you." His look acknowledged the truth. "I'll come for you tomorrow," he said.

She nodded, understanding the blunt, soldierly declaration of intent. And suddenly they were grinning at each other. He lifted her mouth for one more searing kiss, and turned away.

* * * *

Leaving the highwayman's house was easier than Miranda imagined. After a supper of roast chicken and bread, they had dressed as warmly as they could in what was left of their clothes and contrived a way for Nate to tuck his injured arm inside his coat. He fashioned a closed lamp out of a hooded candleholder fitted with a glowing coal from their fire and the stub of a candle. When the house was quiet, they left the pretty room, and Nate reached under the wainscot on the wall to open a concealed jib door to a servants' stair. He lit their lamp, and they descended. The stair ended in a hall lined with the little rooms where the work of the house was done. The hall was lit, so Nate extinguished their candle and drew Miranda along after him.

No one stopped them as they stepped out into the night. Somewhere deep in the house a dog barked once and was silenced. Miranda's heart pounded, and over the beat of it she tried to listen to Nate's breathing. It sounded to her as if he had been running. They had agreed not to speak until they reached the shelter of the trees on either side of the long drive.

Nate led them swiftly across the gravel of the drive, which sounded in Miranda's ears like the crunching of a dog's teeth on bones. She breathed more easily as they crossed the damp grass and stepped into the shadows of the drive. Nate offered her the lamp and took her other hand in his, tugging her along the edge of the drive. His hand felt warm and sweaty in spite of the cold air, and his breath came in pants of exertion. She wanted him to slow down, but their plan depended on reaching the gate under cover of darkness.

In the dark, unseen things reached for her and brushed her bonnet and her face with wet tendrils or snagged and tore at her dress. What had seemed a short distance on the back of the highwayman's horse now seemed an endless march. Her shoes were wet, her toes cold, and her side ached. Traveling with Nate Wilde was decidedly hard on a woman's fashionable appearance, and she would tell him so, just as soon as they reached a comfortable inn.

The faint pale strip of the drive kept them on a straight uphill course. It occurred to Miranda that the drive might be a couple of miles in length. She pushed herself to keep pace with Nate. At last she could see a tiny pinpoint of light that must come from the lodge. She hoped Nate had a plan for dealing with the gatekeeper.

The road took a dip and rose again toward the light. They were close now. Then abruptly Nate's hand slipped from hers, and he crumpled. He hit the ground with a thud. Miranda put down the lamp and reached for him. He was out cold, covered in sweat. She pulled his head and shoulders into her lap. She reached for the lamp, knocked it, and heard it clatter away from her in the dark. They had come so close to the gate.

"Nate Wilde," she whispered. "Wake up."

He didn't stir. His limbs felt lifeless, and the sweat seemed to dry up on his brow. She shoved her hand into his coat and felt for his heart. It still beat.

If she was being punished, the punishment was deserved. She was the one who had flirted with gentlemen in the shop, telling stories of her mother and the shoe buckles. She was the one who had foolishly loved Lord Hazelwood and hidden the note he'd asked her to deliver. Because she'd failed to deliver the note, Jane Fawkener had been kidnapped by the Russian spy Malikov and the club had been closed.

But hadn't her papa shown her Mama's silver buckles and given her Mama's thimble? And was it so wrong to want a mother who'd been brave and clever and escaped the Revolution? And hadn't her mother named her Miranda, who was a duke's daughter in a play?

She hugged Nate tighter.

A heavy hand fell on her shoulder.

Miranda shrieked.

"It's just me, Miranda," said a deep familiar voice, "your amiable and much aggrieved host. After the care I've provided, to go sneaking off in the night? What a troublesome pair you are."

The flare of a lantern illuminated Nate's crumpled form in her lap. Miranda held on tight.

"You have to let go, sweetheart. We have to get him back to the house."

Spirits—those which bubble up in the husband hunter's glass and those which arise spontaneously in her breast—are great provokers of the wrong word. In an instant a thought flashes from her mind to her tongue and cannot be recalled. She stands among her companions with her frailties revealed in a new and glaring light. She must acknowledge the fault and yet take heart. The suitor who abandons her for one piece of folly is not worthy. The mortifying moment of indiscretion will pass and be forgotten by those who understand her character more fully. And every wrong word, except those uttered in spite, may be forgiven.

—*The Husband Hunter's Guide to London*

Chapter 17

Miranda leaned back against the silken headboard and closed her eyes. Just for a minute. She didn't know what else she could do to bring Nate Wilde back to his senses soon.

She had endured their host's scorn and a severe scold from the sturdy maid on the night of their attempted escape. Her shoes and clothes had been beyond saving with mud and tears. She had accepted a cast-off kerseymere gown the color of potatoes and a pair of yellow lady's pumps sadly out of fashion. She ached from bending over Nate to sponge his brow or turn him on his side, or hold his head to pour some draught down his throat. Her hair was lifeless and flat against her scalp. She was out of tooth powder, the borrowed gown smelled a bit lived in, and her hands were raw from washing them every time she tended Nate.

Nothing had gone according to plan. Captain Clare hadn't come for them. Her papa must be most distressed by now to have no word of her. They'd been a burden and an expense to their captor, who had laughed at Miranda's attempt to pay the doctor from the purse Nate carried. She should have stayed at home. She should have accepted that she was a shopkeeper's daughter. Her papa kept an excellent shop on a fashionable street. She should have been content to show gentlemen the elegant brushes and the fragrant lotions, soaps, and balms. She should not have gone dreaming such lofty dreams of being a lady with a fine lord for a husband.

She was not so sure she liked fine lords any longer. Whoever their captor was, he was heartless and mocking. And the worst of it all was that it was all her fault. If she had not broken her promise to Lord Hazelwood, none of this would be happening. The club would be open, Nate would be there making coffee for the spies, and she would be in Papa's shop in her prettiest clothes.

Hot silent tears filled her eyes and ran down her cheeks, and her nose ran, and she felt too tired to care.

"Fine protector I turned out to be." Nate's voice made her open her eyes. His hand, moving across the counterpane, found her knee. "Are you crying?" he asked.

She wiped her arm under her nose. "No. Are you in your senses again?"

"I think so," he said. "How long have I been out?"

"Days."

"Our captor hasn't offered you any insult, has he?"

"As if he would deign to notice a shop girl in a potato sack."

"You're beautiful. Every man notices you." His hand found hers and squeezed. "I missed you."

"You couldn't miss me. You were in a fever."

"I missed you." He laced his fingers with hers.

And Miranda started sobbing, sobbing, sobbing. "You couldn't miss me," she said, coming up on her knees on the bed beside him and looking down into his face. "Because I'm the reason the club closed. I'm the one to blame. I didn't deliver that message from Hazelwood to Jane Fawkener, and she was kidnapped, and Hazelwood fooled the government, and Lord Chartwell shut the club down. It's my fault."

She leaned over him, burying her head against his chest, and felt his good arm come around her, his good hand sweep up and down her back, until the sobs became hiccups.

"You're overset," he said. "You've been taking care of me this whole while, haven't you?"

She nodded against his chest. She had come to know that chest quite well, the simple churchlike symmetry of arching ribs over the hollow of his belly, the surprising soft dark hair around the coins of his nipples and down the center valley of his torso. Because their captor had accepted the story that she was Nate's wife, she'd seen rather more of him than propriety allowed. She found she liked the compact shape of his body, lean and neat, and hard and flat where she was soft and round.

He cleared his throat. "It's time I did something for us, and I promise I won't lead you through the woods again."

Miranda lifted her head. "Did you hear me? I am the one to blame for the club closing."

"I heard you," he said. "Can you help me sit up against some pillows? I'm weak as a cat."

For a few minutes they pushed and pulled pillows and bedclothes until Nate lay back panting against the headboard. "Come here."

Miranda sat back on her bottom and scooted up against the headboard next to him. He lifted his good arm over her shoulders and pulled her tight against him. He had claimed to be so weak, but his arm was lean and hard and strong around her. He turned his head slightly, and his mouth brushed against her forehead.

It was a light touch, sweeter than spun sugar. It made her eyes fill up again and spill down her cheeks.

"You're crying," he said. "It was just a kiss. I didn't think you would mind so much." His hold slackened. He tipped his head back against the headboard.

She glanced at him and watched his throat work as he swallowed.

"I didn't mind," she said, snuggling closer under his arm. "I just thought that it was...that you meant it to be a last kiss."

He opened one eye. "Never."

"You'll kiss me again?"

He smiled. "As soon as you lend me some tooth powder."

"I haven't got any," she said.

He didn't say anything. She sneaked a peek at him. His eyes were closed. His cheeks shadowed with beard. A year earlier he had kissed her for the first time. It had been a revelation, that kiss, but then she'd been so foolish over Lord Hazelwood.

She nudged him. "Does that mean you won't kiss me again?"

"I'll kiss you senseless when I get the chance. If you'll let me." One eye opened. "It's a good thing you came with me, Miranda," he said. "Together, we'll get the club open again. You'll see."

The husband hunter's Season offers such a round of pleasure, activity, and novelty, that she may mistake the dizzying whirl that occupies her for the happiness she seeks. She may, like a child dazzled by gaily wrapped presents and frosted cakes, imagine that these are the source of the gladness she feels in being alive and engaged in her world. But the happiness she seeks in marriage is of a different order entirely. It is the happiness of what is suitable, fitting, and felicitous in the choice of a partner.

—The Husband Hunter's Guide to London

Chapter 18

Lucy looked around the little white-and-blue chapel. She and her friends had attended services together for nearly two years. They sat in their favorite back bench, awaiting the call to rise for the final prayer and recessional hymn. By now Lucy knew many faces in the crowd, and some names. She tried to guess who had left *The Husband Hunter's Guide to London* on the last pew for her friends to find. Everyone in the chapel certainly recognized the group of them as most regular members of the congregation and knew something of their habit of exchanging books each Sunday. Someone had placed the worn blue volume with the water spot on the cover just where Lucy habitually sat. Whom was she to thank? If she understood him at all, Captain Harry Clare was to meet her at the chapel, take her up in his curricle, and propose.

A fortnight had seen this change in them from near strangers passing in her father's inn, to friends who understood each other deeply. It was not only the little book that had helped them, but dear Adam, her first and dearest friend, her playmate, her charge, and some would say, her burden.

Harry Clare's kindness to Adam, his defense of Adam from Findlater, and his understanding that Lucy needed Adam to be kept safe so that she could enjoy London—those were the acts that had first made Lucy see something more in him than the faded glory of his scarlet coat over his broad shoulders. Then she'd seen his other self in town among the fashionable people her friends collected around them and understood his loneliness, his wit, and his sense of duty.

The other, the necessity of being close to his person, of touching and being touched, of sitting in the middle of the bench together rather than at either end, that had come later, somewhat mysteriously, catching her unawares, a thing you could not observe happening, until it had happened, until you were in the midst of it. No other gentleman had awakened her senses as Harry Clare had.

Her book would say that she had permitted liberties, but it had never been a matter of permission, nothing had been unwelcome, she had given as good as she got. If he had more knowledge than she in such matters, he had not pressed her beyond where she was ready to go. The least ladylike of feelings—impatience and greed—had possessed her in those moments. She hardly knew where such feelings came from.

Around her, people stirred. Lucy took up her hymnal and stood. One final song, a few words to friends and acquaintances, and her husband hunting would end. She would be in Harry Clare's curricle, headed for the park, and a new life.

* * * *

Harry saw the sexton open the chapel doors and heard the organist begin the recessional. Lucy and her friends would be the last of the congregation to leave. Their habit of gathering in the rear of the church to exchange the latest novels they'd read always put them behind the rest of the churchgoers. But Harry could afford to be patient. The day was mild. They could roll through the park at a leisurely pace to exchange smiles and vows. He would give her the ring he carried in a box in his coat. He had let go of the case, of his role as a spy, and of the ambition to possess Mountjoy and restore it to its former dignity. All the things he had been fighting for since he'd left the army.

In their place, fate had seen fit to put a girl, a gray-eyed, fair-haired girl with waves of curls and a wide-mouthed, freckle-dusted face. She was loyal and kind, and the warmth of her unaffected laugh drew him as strongly as a fire on a bitter night. If he could not make her "Lady Somebody," he would make her his lady, The Honorable Mrs. Harry Clare. If she wanted to run her inn, he would settle there and make a home in that small patch of England for which, after all, the war with Bonaparte had been fought. If he had to defend her from her unseen enemy, he would do that, too. He patted the ring box in his breast pocket. It was still there.

These satisfying thoughts passed through his mind as the first members of the congregation emerged from the church, blinking in the March sunlight. Separating from the crowd and crossing the street to Harry were his fellow spies and friends, Hazelwood and Blackstone. They came with grave faces and purposeful strides. With the club closed, Harry could not guess the meaning of their coming.

"There you are, Clare," said Hazelwood. "Kirby told us you might be here."

"I'm meeting Miss Holbrook for a drive in the park."

Blackstone nodded. "We thought as much, and regret this errand."

"What's happened?" Harry asked.

"Richard is dead," said Hazelwood.

"Richard?" Harry glanced between their two perfectly sober faces. "Richard is forty-one."

Neither man made a reply, and Harry rallied himself to ask more questions. "How? Where? When?"

The crowd was already thinning in front of the church. Hazelwood was answering Harry's questions, but Harry's blood was pounding in his ears, blocking the words. "Whatever you need, name it," Hazelwood said.

"You are Mountjoy, now," Blackstone said.

And Lucy Holbrook stepped into the sunlight with a quick, light step and shining eyes turned to him.

"Pardon me," Harry said to his friends. "I must speak to someone a moment." He stepped into the street and halted as a carriage rattled past, the driver swerving and shaking a fist at Harry. He tried again with more care and reached Lucy. She extended her gloved hands. He took them in his, regretting the gloves, the street, the glare of day on this meeting.

"I must postpone our drive. Can your friends take you home?"

"Of course. Something has happened." Her hands squeezed his.

"My brother has died. I never..."

"And your friends are here to help you?" she said, glancing at Hazelwood and Blackstone.

"Yes, there are things I must do." He held himself together.

"Then you must do them. Cordelia and Cassandra will take me home."

He nodded. "That will be best," he said. He tried to frame a parting that sounded right, but none came to mind. He could not offer for her now. Mountjoy, that mountain of debt and duty, made him the least eligible man in London.

"Go," she said. "You know where to find me."

He bowed a farewell.

In every enterprise there are expenses that must be borne if the venture is to succeed, and husband hunting is surely a vital venture. The husband hunter, whatever her resources, must invest wisely if she is to reap the benefit of spending a Season in London. If she feels she must economize in any way, let it be in those areas where simplicity serves her aim. If she must invest heavily, let it be in that activity which brings her with consistency to the notice of eligible gentlemen. A box at the Opera House may procure a lifetime of happiness at relatively little cost.

—*The Husband Hunter's Guide to London*

Chapter 19

A box at the opera at forty pounds for the Season was in Cassandra and Cordelia's view a bargain for any woman wishing to secure a husband. Bringing Lucy to the opera near the end of her fortnight in London had been the plan from the beginning. Lucy owed her friends a great deal for their kindness. Without them, she would have forever imagined and perhaps regretted her lost London Season. Now she knew she would have no regrets. A delay in her happiness was inevitable as Harry Clare dealt with his new circumstances, but tonight she would show her friends only smiles.

As they stood in the red-and-gold box before the gaze of hundreds of people, Cordelia said, "This is your send-off, dear girl, your farewell for a time, but we hope you'll return."

"Of course she will," Cassandra said. "Tonight we'll see what her true prospects are. Some gentlemen will merely wave from the pit. Those we can dismiss. But others will rush to our box at the interval. Those we can consider serious suitors."

"Well, we've plenty of room in our box, dear," Cordelia assured her. "We can accommodate half a dozen candidates for your hand easily."

Lucy laughed. "Oh dear, I hope some poor fellow doesn't feel he must propose before all of London." She did not confess that she had no need of dozens of suitors.

Lucy had not seen such a crowd before. She was glad at that moment that most of her evenings had been spent in smaller gatherings. Nearly all of London must be there. Except Captain Clare. Her heart ached for him.

His grief would be the harder to bear than hers had been for the bitterness between the brothers.

Margaret, on Lucy's right, smiled at her. The return of Lady Eliza's son and granddaughter had given her a rare evening away from her duties as companion. "You look lovely, Lucy. I had not guessed when our friends showed me the fabric that pewter would favor you."

"Yes, and how fortunate for me to look well in it. I imagine that if Miss Throckmorton is here in her usual gold, she's in danger of being mistaken for one of the pelmets."

"Ladies," said Cassandra, lifting her glasses to her face to survey the crowd, "do pay attention. I see several gentlemen already eying Lucy."

Lucy was still laughing when she caught a gentleman in a neighboring box staring at her. The gentleman seemed unable to leave off the stare, pronounced and puzzled. He was older than Lucy or her suitors by many years, and she was sure she had not met him at any of the dinner parties she'd attended. Her appearance or her laugh or her very existence seemed to offend him.

The musicians began to play, and the crowd settled into a low murmur as people took seats and turned from each other to the stage in anticipation. Lucy ventured one last glance at the staring man. He looked away when she caught him at it. Margaret noted him as well.

"Who is that gentleman?" she asked. "Do you know?"

"I believe its young Lydford. How odd of him, and I dare say, rude, to stare so. Do you know him?"

Lucy shook her head. "Should I? Is he the disapproving father of some young gentleman of my acquaintance?"

Margaret shook her head. "His only son is betrothed."

The first part of the program passed quickly. It was a light piece with a pair of sopranos who were favorites with the lively crowd. Lucy endeavored simply to let the music transport her, joining in the laughter and applause. It was easier to forget the scowling gentleman in the neighboring box than to stop looking for Captain Clare.

At the interval, the audience, as if weary of being contained on benches for an hour, took to its feet. Lucy's friends became quite businesslike.

"Now, we shall see," said Cassandra.

A servant was dispatched for refreshments, and the ladies arranged themselves to greet callers to their box. And they came. Not Lucy's baron, or the brilliant inventor, but several dashing men of fashion, in their black evening clothes and their easy charming ways, and yet there was no seriousness in any of them. They were playing at courtship.

Lucy relaxed at once. Her secret happiness would not wound another. No one would make an awkward proposal she was compelled to reject. She smiled at the man in front of her and sipped the lemon water he'd procured and waited for the interval to end.

Before it did, however, there was an interruption. The disapproving gentleman entered their box. He greeted Cassandra and Cordelia with a curt bow and demanded, "Who is your protégé?"

Margaret stepped into the shocked silence, making the presentation. "Mr. John Lydford, Miss Lucy Holbrook."

Lucy made her curtsy. The gentleman seemed to be experiencing a strong emotion.

"You are not with your parents?" he asked.

"They are not alive," she said. "I'm here with my good friends, as you see."

"But who were your parents?" he insisted.

"See here, sir," said Lucy's lemon water–procuring companion. "You've no call to badger Miss Holbrook about her connections. She's a woman of property, and I dare say, as well born as any of us."

Mr. Lydford quelled him with a fierce glare, and Lucy put a hand on her companion's sleeve. It was clear that Mr. Lydford was laboring under some misapprehension.

"My father was Thomas Holbrook of St. Botolph's. You would not know him, Mr. Lydford, unless you were, many years ago, a follower of the fancy and knew him as Iron Tom."

Mr. Lydford's brow contracted in a frown of puzzlement. "But how did you come by that laugh?"

"Oh dear. I couldn't say. We laughed often in our house. I am sorry my parentage disappoints you, sir."

* * * *

The party gathered around the tea tray after the opera was not a lively one. Harry Clare had left no message at the house. Lucy rallied herself to show a cheerful spirit in spite of the uneasiness she felt in not hearing from him. After all a delay in embarking on an outing of pleasure was as common as clouds in an English sky. She could wait a few days or weeks before she set out for a lifetime of happiness.

Margaret was enjoying the last few minutes among them before she returned to her duties as a companion. Lucy and Margaret sat together while Cordelia served the tea and Cassandra managed the conversation, turning it to Captain Clare.

"So now he is the Earl of Mountjoy. It will be a terrible burden for him," Cassandra predicted.

Cordelia agreed. "His brother's affairs were quite tangled I understand, and his debts, staggering."

"You said he had friends with him, did you not, Lucy?" Margaret asked.

Lucy nodded. She did not trust herself to speak. The sisters' words cast a shadow of doubt on her happiness. She hoped it would be a fleeting one.

Cassandra changed the subject. "We might have been overly sanguine about your prospects, but you are now established here with a circle of friends and may return at any time. We'll see you betrothed yet."

"Thank you, Cassandra."

"We have been so glad to have you with us, dear girl," Cordelia seconded her sister. "You must come again, later in the Season, when you feel that you can. Then we shall see who offers for you."

Lucy promised she would. Then perhaps she would have glad news of a betrothal to share. For a few minutes they had little else to say.

Late as the hour was, the bell rang, and the butler, waiting up to see Margaret off, came a few minutes later to announce that the Earl of Mountjoy was below and wishful of a word with Miss Holbrook.

Lucy descended, her spirits rising, instantly glad that he could think of her at all in such a time. The butler had shown him into the morning room. A branch of candles on the table made a circle of light that just illuminated him in a sober suit of mourning.

It might be the light or the shock he was under, but she had never seen him look so distant from her, not even early in their acquaintance. The sisters' words about his situation now seemed ominous. "What is it? Have you had more bad news?"

"Miss Holbrook," he began, and she reached out a hand, but when he made no move to take it, she placed it on the table to steady herself at the formality of it. "The change in my circumstances means I will be weeks if not months trying to sort out Richard's affairs."

She nodded. Apparently, they were not to touch tonight.

"You will return to the inn?"

"You needn't worry. Cassandra and Cordelia will take me tomorrow. Only I must trouble you for one favor." She lifted her chin to face him squarely.

"Yes."

"You've kept Adam safe, but now I must ask you to bring him to me."

"As you wish, but I must ask a favor in return."

She waited with no idea of what he could mean. He was grieving and troubled, but he'd changed toward her in some way she could not understand.

"Will you consent to try to unlock Adam's memory?"

"Now?"

"He may be able to identify his enemy."

"And you suspect that Adam's enemy will act against him?"

"You cannot protect yourself...or Adam against the man if you do not know who he is."

And you will not be there to protect me, she thought. "I will not be alone," she said.

"I have a second motive for asking this of you. Two young friends of mine are missing. They were taken during the most recent robbery of one of Radcliffe's Rockets."

"Taken?"

"The guard wounded my friend."

"The youth with the teeth and ears?"

"Nate Wilde."

Lucy sat down. "What can that have to do with Adam?"

"The inn is watched. Most likely Adam's enemy sent Findlater and... took the cat."

"Queenie was taken?"

"I suspect so. Without her, Adam loses an early warning of approaching danger."

"How can Adam have such a terrible enemy? Adam, harmless Adam?"

"Likely, Miss Holbrook, he witnessed a murder."

She shivered at it, and at his tone. How had she become Miss Holbrook again? But what he said changed everything. He was not after all a man taken with a girl's charms and wooing her, he was someone else entirely. "You have been less than honest with me from the start, Cap—what do I call you now?"

"Mountjoy," he said.

"From the start you have befriended us, not out of kindness or sympathy or affection, but as part of...what?"

"An investigation. A case. For the Foreign Office. Likely the person whose murder Adam witnessed was a British agent carrying important papers as well as money."

"By agent, you mean spy." She looked up and met his gaze. "You are a spy."

"I am."

Lucy stood again and backed away from him. "When did you plan to tell me?"

He didn't answer. He did not extend a hand or take a step in her direction. He offered no excuse, no comfort. He had been content to play with her happiness, to lead her to betray herself with feelings she believed he returned in equal measure.

She had mistaken his intentions from the first. The happiness she had looked for not hours earlier was a lie. Her legs grew weak, her stomach churned, and she knew she must end the interview at once or disgrace herself.

She did not extend a hand again. There would be no parting touch. "I doubt we will meet again," she said. She did not know what name to call him. "You have my sincerest sympathy on the loss of your brother and my gratitude for your care of Adam in this fortnight. Good night."

She turned away and slipped through the door as quickly as she could.

The husband hunter may wonder at the models of marriage she sees before her in London society. Seeing couples whose glittering nuptials were the talk of town a year or two earlier barely exchange a civil word in company or speak only in such commonplaces as to suggest a dull familiarity with each other's thoughts may lead the husband hunter to doubt the possibility of happiness in marriage. She must not let public moments of irritation or indifference between married persons of her acquaintance diminish her faith in the happiness that awaits her in the union of true hearts.

—*The Husband Hunter's Guide to London*

Chapter 20

Early in the morning Nate and Miranda were summoned to a large dim salon with red-damasked walls. Velvet drapery kept out most of the light. The walls were hung with pictures of martyrs and madonnas, all of whom wore fewer clothes than seemed saintly or even proper to Nate. He knew what it felt like to be near naked around the woman he loved. It was not a saintly feeling. Their host lay on his back on a gold velvet sofa as long as a Thames barge, looking at the ceiling.

"You look reasonably recovered from your wounds," he said, glancing at Nate, where he and Miranda stood hand in hand, facing their host.

With any luck Nate would convince the highwayman to let them return to the Tooth and Nail. He had instructed Miranda to let him do the talking. "Where we are?" he asked.

"You're at Lyndale Abbey. You've been my guests. Anything to complain of?"

"Nothing, sir," Miranda said.

Nate elbowed her in the ribs. Not five minutes into the conversation, and she was breaking the rules.

She elbowed him back. "We owe you my husband's life."

"You owe me a bit of truth, I'd say." The highwayman swung his long legs to the floor and came upright. Even seated, he was a tall man. "What's your connection to Harry Clare?"

Miranda drew a quick breath at the captain's name.

Nate squeezed her hand to steady her. "We work for him, sir. He asked us to investigate a former footman from Hartwood Manor. We were returning from our investigation when the Rocket was stopped. We're grateful for your assistance and don't wish to trouble you further." He'd rehearsed that line and hoped it was truth enough for the highwayman without giving away the whole.

Their host appeared to consider his own well-polished boots at the end of his very long legs. The pause was disconcerting. The man was obviously thinking. When he looked up again, his dark gaze was sharp but also amused.

"Not the whole story," he said.

Again, Miranda sucked in a telltale breath, and Nate steeled himself, running through possible answers in his head. He'd obviously lost some quickness of wit while he'd lain in bed with a fever.

"Captain Clare came looking for us, didn't he?" Miranda blurted. She bounced a little on her toes.

Their highwayman host grinned. He probably appreciated Miranda's bounce, just as Nate always did.

"I knew he would," she said.

"I wonder then," said their host, "that you tried to leave Lyndale in the middle of the night, on foot, while your...husband still suffered from a bullet wound." The highwayman rose, fixing his gaze on Nate.

He really was a tall fellow. "Apparently, you were to meet Captain Clare at the Tooth and Nail. Is that right?"

Nate nodded. He was glad the highwayman had met Harry Clare. That meant the man knew they were not entirely defenseless.

"If you've recovered sufficiently to endure the jostling of a carriage ride, let's return you to the Tooth and Nail. This investigation of yours intrigues me."

Again Nate nodded. They'd got their wish to return to the inn, but they'd be bringing a curious and not altogether predictable gentleman with them. He'd like to be sure Captain Clare would be there to meet them at the other end.

"Sir, may we send an express to my...wife's father? I have the blunt to pay for it." Nate reached for the leather pouch he'd hung around his neck.

The highwayman waved away the offered money. "Send directly. We leave within the hour." He strode off.

* * * *

Lucy sat next to Adam on his bench with a basket of worn linens beside her and her needle in hand. Lamb and rosemary from the kitchen mingled with pipe smoke and ale from the tap and quite erased from Lucy's memory the delicate scents of Brook Street. Loud talk and laughter from the bench sitters filled her ears. Everything and nothing was the same. She herself was different. More different than she ever imagined.

She had a letter in her pocket from her father's solicitor. It had been waiting for her at the inn with a bundle of things her father had wanted her to have. Her father had never married. There was no Mrs. Holbrook, no mother who had died giving birth to Lucy.

A long, thin envelope had slipped from the solicitor's bundle. Inside was a receipt. At first she could make little sense of the names on the paper. Then she understood. It was a receipt for the portrait of her lady. Her papa had paid the artist the shocking amount of four hundred pounds for a painting of a stranger, and apparently not even an English stranger. The lady's name was *Madame La Comtesse de la Neuvillette*.

One didn't question love. Papa loved her, and Adam loved her. She had never doubted either of them. She had never longed for a mother while she was so loved. But Papa's desire that she become a lady went far beyond what she'd imagined. That her frugal papa, who economized on candles and coal and made sure not to be cheated with a hollow cheese or sprouted malt, could spend so staggering a sum on a painting was a wonder. The day he'd hung the painting in her room, he'd urged her to think of her lady as a friend and model. "Whatever they say at your school," he'd told her, "about your papa, know that your lady is on your side."

Papa's extravagant faith in the portrait of a foreign countess and his utter silence about her real mother now struck her as ominous. All those years ago Amelia had suggested that Lucy was better off knowing nothing about her mother, and perhaps it was true.

The thread that had connected her to the Tooth and Nail had been snipped, as easily and finally as she herself snipped the thread at the end of her needle. Adam sat calmly beside her, polishing candlesticks. Earlier he had repeated his question about the missing Queenie until Lucy thought she must lose all patience with him. His fortnight in London had not harmed him, but it had made her forget the old habit of talking with him. It required the patience of needlework, the steady repetition of even stitches, the careful piecing together of parted seams, and a willingness to break off threads going nowhere.

This morning she had set herself the task of mending table linens. Later she must face the account books. She drew another cloth from her basket, held it up to the light, and discovered a gravy stain the size of a butter dish. She turned the cloth several ways, but the stain could not be concealed. She put aside her thimble and needle and began to tear the ruined linen into strips.

Her people had welcomed her home. Mrs. Vell made a treacle tart, the bench sitters toasted her with their ale, Will Wittering grinned at her, and Hannah babbled for an hour about all that happened in her absence. It was Hannah's account of the inn that now troubled Lucy. In spite of Queenie's mysterious absence, the inn remained as it had always been, comfortable and warm, and noisy. In the midst of the daily comings and goings of neighbors and guests, she could not credit Mountjoy's warning of danger from spies and murderers. What did spies have to do with the Tooth and Nail? But all morning Adam had repeated his question about Queenie, and a thing that Hannah said stuck in Lucy's mind. A fine gentleman had come to the inn every afternoon while Lucy was away. He was the one who had come once, before Lucy had left for London, the gentleman who had ordered a fish dinner and disappeared without eating it. When Lucy had asked Hannah what sort of gentleman he was, Hannah told her he was a gentleman doctor, with a fine coat and hat and a black bag. Hannah was sure he would come again and glad for the coin he gave her each time he came. She promised to be on the lookout for him.

Mountjoy had told Lucy the inn was watched. She had not asked him how he knew or what that meant. A fish-ordering gentleman who skipped without paying did not seem like a potential enemy, but a doctor who came every day and went out of his way to befriend Hannah bothered her.

She wanted to rail at Mountjoy for cutting up her peace, for disconnecting her from the familiar world in which she belonged. She, who had been content to dream of being a lady, had had a taste of it now. She had opened the box of London pleasures, beside which the pleasures of the Tooth and Nail looked small and shabby, everything plain, worn, and loud. Doors banged and men shouted. She, Iron Tom's daughter, was someone else, someone she didn't know. She had only Adam left to connect her to the inn. She had believed his past to be past, and yet apparently it was present, and what little she had, what she was left with after the London dream crumbled, could be taken away from her.

She would not let that happen. She would fight it. On one point she and Mountjoy had agreed. He thought, as she had thought years earlier, that Adam's sayings made sense, told a story, and that unraveling the story might help Adam overcome the past. She looked at her childhood companion now. He was not as calm as he first appeared. In Queenie's absence, his hands paused in their work every few minutes, and he tilted his head to listen to the sounds of the inn as if there might be something amiss. He was not in distress, just slightly unsettled. If there ever were a moment to try to help him, it was now before Hannah's gentleman doctor returned.

"Adam." She put a hand on his sleeve. "Will you come with me to Papa's room?"

He put aside his polish and his rags and took her hand. They made their way to the back of the inn, and Lucy let them into the familiar room. Adam turned as if to go to his bed under the stairs, but Lucy steered him to her papa's chair. She lit the lamps that Adam never needed.

Once she had him seated, she was not sure how to proceed. "We're going to have a talk, Adam," she told him. "Here in this safe place, about what happened to you long ago when you came to the inn."

"Adam stayed," he said.

Lucy took a steadying breath. "I know you did, Adam, and Geoffrey ran away."

Adam began to tremble, shaking his head from side to side. "No, no, no, no, no," he murmured.

Lucy knelt at his feet and took his large, familiar hands firmly in hers. "A terrible thing happened, Adam, but we are going to face it. We're going to name it. We are not going to be afraid any longer."

He stopped his murmuring, his head tilted to listen to her.

Lucy gave his hands one last squeeze and rose and crossed to her father's wardrobe, taking the key from the ring at her waist, kneeling, and opening the drawer where her father had long ago put away her list of Adam's words.

The key turned. The drawer was stuffed and the wood swollen with age, but as Lucy pulled, it came open. Her father had saved a sheer white dress with raised dots, a sampler with her first alphabet in colored stitches, a package of her letters to him from school, a lock of her hair, a bundle of school bills, and a pair of tiny shoes. There was an old quilt and a limbless doll. Everything smelled of cedar and lavender and long ago. There was nothing to answer her suddenly pressing questions about her mother.

She pulled the letters into her lap and untied the ribbon around them. These were her letters from school, but the list she'd made of Adam's words was not among them. She put them aside and dug deeper into the drawer. An old edition of the peerage made her shake her head. Her father had so wanted her to be a lady. She put aside a primer she remembered as one of her first books, another book of the *Adventures of Tom True,* and a box of pencils and chalks. She was sure she had watched her father put her list of Adam's sayings in this very drawer.

Beneath the books lay another bundle wrapped in thin, yellowing crepe, the fabric brittle at the edges as she lifted the bundle from the drawer and set it aside on the rug. There was no sign of her list at the bottom of the drawer, only the faint smell of cedar and old things. She had counted on her list, sure that if she could see it again, she would discern the order in the narrative that she had missed as a child.

She pulled the bundle into her lap and began to unfold the crepe. Adam stirred slightly. "Adam stayed," he said.

In the folds of fabric she found the white lace cap of a child of perhaps two and a white knitted mitten for a tiny hand. Beneath the cap and mitten was a gown of the finest white muslin, elegantly embroidered. She unfolded the gown, and stopped, shocked by a long brown stain from the smocking to the hem. She put the garment aside and unfolded the last item in the bundle, a child's coat in pale blue wool with knotted silk embroidery to match the gown, stained with the same terrible dark stain.

She knew with utter certainty that her father had hidden these things to keep them secret because they had come with Adam to the inn. Adam had brought them from the terrible scene he had witnessed. An image that could not be stopped sprang into her mind of Adam holding a bleeding child. He had held Lucy often enough as a girl. She knew his strength and the way he cradled her in his arms. She had always felt protected in his hold.

She laid the dress and coat back in the yellowing crepe and put the bundle next to the other things she had taken from the drawer. Lined up across the floor they made a sort of history from the most recent items in her life, her letters from school, to items from perhaps before her life, from Adam's arrival at the inn. She shook each one to see whether it might hold the missing list, but she didn't find it.

"Adam." She turned to him. "You must help me. I know it hurts to remember. I will ask only this one time." She laid the child's clothes in his lap.

His hands closed around the folds of the tiny garments. His body began to tremble.

"Tell me, Adam," she said.

His throat worked. His nose ran. He lifted the clothes to his chest and held them there. "Mr. Tom say Adam not talk. Not tell."

Lucy stood and put her hands on his shoulders. "It's time now, Adam. Talk to me. Talk to Lucy."

With a violent shudder he began to speak. "Adam take Lucy to the bulrushes. Adam stay. Geoffrey ran away. Adam saw. No, no, no, no, no! Adam go."

His head fell forward on his chest. She wiped his running nose with her pinny and rocked him gently. The story was still incomplete. There was nothing about the child. And the bulrushes made no sense. She closed Adam's fist around the baby gown in his arms. "Did you bring the baby to the inn?" she asked him.

"Adam bring Lucy to the inn," he said, nodding emphatically.

The words stunned her. She could not have heard him right, but he repeated them, as was his way. "Adam bring Lucy to the inn. Mr. Tom promise keep her safe. Adam stay. Not talk. Not tell."

The remnants of her childhood lying on the rug told the story in their own way. She was not Tom Holbrook's daughter. Adam had brought her to the inn in bloodied garments, and Tom Holbrook had hidden them both, protected them. It was Adam's blood on the baby clothes. She shuddered, understanding why Mountjoy feared for them, because Adam had not been blind. Whatever he had seen was locked in his mind, tormenting him.

Lucy took the bloodied clothes from his hands and returned the items to the drawer. She wet a cloth and washed his face. There was one more question she had to ask him. "Adam, what did you see?"

In a perilous Season there is one painful difficulty the husband hunter may face, which a thorough sense of duty compels this writer to reveal. From time to time it happens that—from reckless inattention to circumstances, indifference to the world's opinion, or precipitate intimacy without true knowledge of one another's character—two people who appear headed with all possible dispatch for the altar must sever their connection. For the husband hunter it appears that her Season has ended in failure. Nothing could be further from the truth. As painful as is the discovery that she and one particular gentleman do not suit, it marks the beginning of her path to true happiness. The necessity of continuing her engagements, appearing in society, and of meeting from time to time her lost love with some semblance of composure demands the greatest exertions of spirit and courage, but leads inevitably to a healed heart.

—The Husband Hunter's Guide to London

Chapter 21

Harry stood outside of Richard's London house, looking across the square, his friend Blackstone beside him. The air of a London street, for all the effluvia of dirt and smoke wafted into the mix, smelled sweeter and fresher than the stale interior of his dead brother's house.

Harry's other friend Hazelwood had gone round to the mews to summon Harry's carriage and Blackstone's horse. His friends had not left him alone since they'd brought him the news of Richard's death. Together they'd faced Richard's wasted body and sent it on its way to Mountjoy for burial. Together they'd routed the duns gathered at Richard's door and listened to the solicitor's bleak appraisal of Richard's affairs. With Blackstone and Hazelwood at his side, Harry appeared to be up in his count of brothers, having gained two for the one he'd lost.

It was a dry, cold day with a stiff breeze that bent the daffodils in the park low to the ground, bright as the brief dream of Lucy Holbrook as his wife. He had escaped Mountjoy as a boy; now, ironically, Mountjoy had taken hold of him, got him by the throat and wouldn't let go.

"You know," said Blackstone at his side, "you can't let Richard's folly rule your life."

Hazelwood returned and glanced at the two of them. "You know what we need to do," he said.

"Break a few heads?" Blackstone referred to Hazelwood's usual style of dealing with troubles.

Hazelwood grinned. "Always a pleasure. However, I was thinking that we need to get the club reopened. Clare—pardon me, Mountjoy—cannot stay in this cesspit while he settles Richard's affairs. He needs good coffee, and he needs to be paid. What was that case you were working on, the blind man? Let's solve it."

"When?" Blackstone asked.

"Now, of course," said Hazelwood. "Where's the blind man, Mountjoy? Some inn, right?"

"The Tooth and Nail," Harry said, "but..."

A pair of grooms brought round Hazelwood's curricle and Blackstone's horse. Hazelwood was instantly in motion. "Should we be armed?"

Harry had no time to answer before another carriage drew up, a high perch phaethon driven by their leader, Goldsworthy. The big man on top of such a vehicle was a sight to see. Next to him, clinging to the side of the carriage, was Kirby, waving an express.

"There you are, Cap—my lord. They're alive. I've had an express. They return today to the Tooth and Nail."

Goldsworthy looked down at Harry. "You've been holding out on me, lad. You had your blind man under my nose for a fortnight. Now we'll see what he has to say." He set his horses in motion, and the curricle rattled off.

For a moment none of the three friends moved. The sight of the big man perched atop the elegant vehicle instead of behind his enormous desk stunned Harry.

Hazelwood voiced the thought in Harry's mind. "Rather cares about this case, doesn't he?"

Blackstone raised one dark brow. "I think that's our cue, gentlemen."

* * * *

Hannah's knock on the door roused Lucy from her thoughts. Adam lay asleep on his bed under the stairs, exhausted from telling the story. Lucy now knew something of the horror he had seen, though she was far from understanding the why of it.

"Miss, miss," Hannah called through the door. "The gray doctor is here. He's in the private dining room, like 'e likes. I asked 'is name, but he told me not to be 'pertinent. He's asking for you, miss."

"I'll be with him directly," she told Hannah. "You're to stay with Adam."

Hannah's eyes grew wide. She did not like to be around him when he had one of his episodes. "He's asleep, Hannah. He just needs to hear your voice if he wakes, to know that he's safe."

Hannah bobbed a curtsy.

Lucy removed her pinny and crossed the inn. It was the quiet time of day between the breakfast sitting and the afternoon stage. Mrs. Vell was off to feed her own family. Frank must be in the brew house or the cellars, checking his lines or his supplies. The bench sitters were at work.

Lucy knocked on the door of the private dining room, and a curiously flat voice bid her enter.

Lucy could see why Hannah had struggled to describe the gentleman she saw. His suit of superfine gray wool was smooth, his colorless face, wrinkled like the flesh of a softening apple. He must have been fair in youth, but the gold of his hair and brows had faded to ash. Pale waves of that hair swept back from a high brow. The burgundy silk of his waistcoat and gold of his watch fob spoke of prosperity. She judged him to be fifty or more. He stood at the table, his hands resting on a black medical bag.

His pale blue eyes widened when she greeted him.

"Good afternoon, Miss Holbrook," he said. "Permit me to introduce myself. I am Doctor Waller. I've come for Adam Pickersgill."

"Come for Adam?"

"Perhaps you've been expecting me. Your father made provision in his will for Adam to be cared for at Normand House. You've heard of it, of course, a private asylum, a superior establishment for the care of persons suffering from imbalances of every sort."

"I beg your pardon but I know of no plans my father made for Adam to leave the Tooth and Nail."

"Ah," said the doctor, "you had a careful father." He looked at Lucy as if she were a puzzle. "Knowing that your circumstances would change and that as a woman of property you would look to marry, your father wished to relieve you of the burden of Adam's care."

"Thank you," she said. "But whatever provisions my father made for Adam can wait. At present I have no plans to marry, or to leave the inn. You may leave your card should you wish me to seek your assistance at any time later."

"I beg your pardon, perhaps the confidences of little Hannah, so eager to please, have misled me. I have my bag here, however." He snapped open the leather physician's case. "Would it be possible for me to examine Adam today for future reference? Then we will know what regimen of care would best suit him at Normand House."

Lucy shook her head. "I'm afraid another day will have to do. Adam is asleep at present."

The doctor looked disappointed. He stared into his case. "Well," he said, "perhaps you'd be willing to answer a few questions. He's quite blind, is he? How frequent are his episodes of rage?"

"Rage? Doctor, I'm sorry, but I cannot help you. As Adam is not your patient, it is inappropriate for us to have any conversation about his condition. I must ask you to leave now."

"That, I cannot do, Miss Holbrook, not without Adam." The doctor drew a pistol from his bag and leveled it at her.

However agreeable or disagreeable the nature of her family home, the husband hunter has ties of long standing to the friends and relations of her childhood. Sometimes her greatest loyalty and strongest love is reserved for those persons most difficult to love and most demanding of her care and attention. Seeking her own happiness in the face of such ties can seem the worst sort of disloyalty. To free herself from those constraining ties without a wrenching break injurious to all is the business of her Season in London. Her happiness depends upon it.

—The Husband Hunter's Guide to London

Chapter 22

With a pistol at her back Lucy led Waller out of the private dining room, down the stairs, past Harry Clare's Waterloo case, and across the empty common room. Frank had not returned to the tap, and no sounds came from the kitchen. Lucy moved carefully and as slowly as she could.

Waller continued to talk. "You will bring the old fool to my carriage. We will go out through the kitchen."

"Who are you?" she asked. He wasn't a doctor.

A sharper poke in the back was her answer.

As they entered the passageway to her father's room, Waller said, "You should thank me, girl. If you do nothing stupid, you'll be free of your troublesome madman."

Lucy stopped at her father's door and called Hannah to open it.

"You know what to do," Waller told Lucy.

Hannah opened the door, and Waller shoved Lucy forward, grabbing Hannah by the arm and putting the pistol to her head. Hannah froze in his hold, her eyes wide, her mouth opening and closing in a soundless cry.

Lucy turned to Adam sleeping on his bed. She let her gaze sweep over the room. She could see no weapon, nothing to use against the doctor, who was no doctor.

For a few minutes she concentrated on Adam, waking him with familiar words and gestures. It took a while to get him fully awake and upright. She ventured a glance at Hannah silently shaking, tears running down her face, her hands clutching her pinny.

At last she got Adam to his feet, and he began to shuffle toward the door holding her arm. She glanced at the clock steadily marking the time, when she wanted it to hurry, wanted the hands to spin forward so that Frank and Mrs. Vell and the bench sitters would return.

At the door Adam paused and cocked his head, the way he did when he became aware of other persons near him.

"Hannah's waiting for us," Lucy told him. "We're going to go for a walk."

Still Adam didn't move. He was listening, cautiously testing the darkness. She expected an angry outburst from their enemy. His face was full of contempt and impatience. But he only kept the pistol to Hannah's head and the cruel grip on her arm.

"Come on, Adam," Lucy said. "Hannah can't stand idle all day."

Adam moved through the door, and Lucy led him down the passageway with Waller and Hannah behind them. Adam paused to listen intently every few steps. When they reached the empty common room, Lucy ventured a glance back at Hannah.

With a jerk of his head Waller indicated that Lucy was to turn toward the kitchen. It struck her that he didn't speak. He'd had so much to say to her in the private dining room, smooth lies about her father's will and being a doctor. But he had not spoken again since the door of her father's room opened. She understood. Adam might be blind, but he could hear. Adam knew the man's voice. This was the enemy Mountjoy had warned her of. If Lucy could get the man to speak, Adam would not move another step. But if Lucy provoked the false doctor, he might shoot Hannah. Adam's bench was just ahead of them. Once they rounded the bench, they would be out of the sight of anyone entering the inn. All hope of help would be lost. She had to decide.

Behind her the inn door banged open. A deep male voice with a gentlemanly accent called out, "Hallo, innkeeper!"

Adam froze at Lucy's side. Waller slipped behind Lucy into the passageway.

"You there, a little help," called the voice. Boots coming their way sounded against the slate.

"Miss Holbrook?" called another man's voice, younger and less deep.

Lucy turned to face the newcomers, trying to keep her expression calm. A very tall gentleman in a greatcoat, accompanied by Harry Clare's young friend with a bandaged shoulder and a very pretty girl, stood watching her.

At her back Waller hissed, "Put them off. Send them to the private dining room."

At the sound of his voice Adam began to shake all over with the signs of a coming episode. "Geoffrey ran away," he cried. His fists clenched. His arm slipped from Lucy's hold, flying upward with a sudden jerk, unbalancing her.

She staggered against the wall as he began to flail. Waller stepped back, and Hannah slipped from his grasp. She ran straight for the tall gentleman, barreling into him, and clung sobbing to his coat. His arms came around the frightened girl.

Waller recovered, grabbed Lucy, and jammed his pistol against her side.

Behind them, blocking the passageway, Adam flailed and cried out.

Waller yelled at him. "You fool, move."

Adam swung his fist in a wide arc, and Waller inched Lucy farther into the room.

"Nobody takes what's mine. Least of all you. Fool, you should have run, instead of standing like a blinking idiot, staring at your betters. You deserved to have your damned eyes poked."

* * * *

Harry looked across the common room at the raging man holding a pistol to Lucy's side and ruled out reasoning with him. Geoffrey Radcliffe had the eyes of a cornered rat. Keeping his gaze on Lucy, willing her to understand him, Harry wrapped his coat around his elbow, smashed the glass of the Waterloo case at his side, and pulled his sword from the display. He drew the blade from the scabbard with a satisfying scrape of metal on metal. The grip felt right in his hand, the sword an extension of his arm and his will.

He stepped down into the common room, moving purposefully. Ajax Lynley cast him a rueful glance, his arms full of a sobbing girl. Nate Wilde nodded, standing at Lynley's side, shielding Miranda behind him, his shoulder bandaged. Harry saw no sign that Radcliffe had accomplices, a troubling lack since it meant the man's desperation would be greater.

"Geoffrey Radcliffe," he said. He saw Lucy's eyes widen as she realized who her captor was. "Look around you at this piece of England that men fought for, and bled for, and died for."

Radcliffe's gray face contorted in contempt.

"Men you betrayed when you sold England's secrets to her enemies."

"England's still here. His royal fatness is still on the throne."

On Harry's orders Hazelwood had gone to the back of the inn, while Blackstone watched the front door. Harry just needed a little time. Adam was moaning now, still waving his fists. Time to call Adam back to the present.

"Adam," he called. "It's Captain Clare. Lucy needs your help."

Harry waited for the words to reach Adam to snap him out of the past. "Can you drop to your knees when I say so?"

Radcliffe laughed. "You think the fool can help you? What's he good for? What has he ever been good for? Stroking the cat and polishing boots? Let me tell you what a fine help he was, blubbering and crying and letting the Frog have his mistress until the Frenchie poked his eyes out."

Harry's hand tightened on his sword, but he kept his concentration on Adam. He had the old man's attention now. Tremors shook him, but he cocked his head, listening. Lucy stood still and proud in Radcliffe's hold, her golden head held high. Harry's gaze narrowed briefly to her, nothing else. She was his England.

"Sweet on the girl, are you, Captain?" Radcliffe taunted. "I'm taking her. If anyone tries to stop me, she dies."

Harry shook his head. Behind him the inn door opened again. A cold stir of March air passed through the room. Radcliffe glanced up, startled by whatever he saw behind Harry.

Heavy footsteps crunched the broken glass of the Waterloo case. A deep rumbling voice called out, "Radcliffe, you dog. You'll hang for treason."

The pistol in Radcliffe's hand wobbled, and he steadied it, shoving the muzzle deeper against Lucy's side.

Harry's fist clenched the sword grip. He moved forward at an unhurried pace, drawing Radcliffe's gaze back to him. "You have one shot, Radcliffe. You'd best hit me, or you die here."

Again Radcliffe's pistol hand wavered. He edged back, dragging Lucy with him. Behind them in the shadowy passageway Adam stood like a blasted tree.

"Drop, Adam," Harry yelled.

Adam dropped. Radcliffe stumbled back, falling as the backs of his knees collided with Adam's bulk. Radcliffe's arm jerked away from Lucy. She slid to the floor in the instant the pistol discharged.

The ball grazed Harry's ribs as he lunged, caught in the detachment of battle, neither hatred nor fury, but clarity, the smell of powder and blood filling his senses. Momentum drove his sword through Radcliffe's chest. He pulled back as Radcliffe crumpled, curling around the wound, in his eyes the knowledge of death. Then he fell.

* * * *

Lucy scrambled to her feet and went to Harry. He dropped the bloody sword with a clang and took her in his arms, nestling her head under his chin. Around them there seemed to be a great deal of movement and shouting. He was warm and solid and breathing. His lips brushed her forehead. "I couldn't lose you," he said.

"He shot you," she said, lifting her head from his chest.

"Grazed me. I'll have a bruised rib is all." His eyes had an absurdly joyful look.

She watched Harry's friend pull Radcliffe's body off Adam. The large man who had called Radcliffe a dog came to stand over the dead man.

"You probably wanted him alive," Harry said.

The big man shook his great shaggy head. "No. I didn't know his name, didn't know the cheeky devil was hiding in our midst behind a mask of respectability, but I have wanted him dead for twenty years."

Harry's friend helped Adam to his feet. Lucy touched Harry's sober face and went to take Adam's hand and lead him to his bench. Around them she heard familiar voices speaking in shocked tones. The quiet hour had ended. The inn's usual people were returning.

One of Harry's friends organized a small party of bench sitters to move Radcliffe's body. His other friend pulled chairs into a circle around the hearth. Frank Blodget began to pour ale. Mrs. Vell muttered about divine wrath and pork and marched a quietly weeping Hannah off to her kitchen.

"Pardon me." Harry's chestnut-haired friend interrupted. "Blackstone and I will keep the authorities occupied while you all get your story straight. By the way, does the physician's case in the dining room have any bearing on the case?"

Lucy shuddered. "Radcliffe came for Adam, calling himself a Doctor Waller with a private asylum in Fulham. He kept the pistol in the case."

The big man with the head of russet hair like a lion's mane and the look of a large oak tree came to stand before Lucy and Adam. Tears ran down his craggy cheeks.

"Dear, dear girl, your mother is avenged."

"You knew my mother?"

"Oh yes. The countess was fierce and fearless with a laugh no man could resist. She was one of the best agents England ever had."

Lucy turned to Harry, the spy, the man of duty and mission. "You knew?"

"I suspected." His face had the bleak look she remembered from when they parted in the breakfast room at Brook Street.

She turned back to the big man. "You called her 'the countess'?"

"Yes, her French title from her husband—de Neuvillette. He was captured in France. She was on her way to help him escape with funds and documents when she disappeared."

Lucy started. It was the name of the woman in her painting. Her father had not spent wildly on a portrait. He had known who her real mother was. "But she was English?"

"To the core. Penelope Lydford before she married. Of Hartwood."

The bandaged youth, whom Lucy had seen earlier with Harry, now stepped forward, a pretty girl clinging to his good arm. "Hartwood is where Adam came from, sir. Miranda and I confirmed it with Adam's old friend Nanny Ragley. There was a second footman there named Geoffrey Gibbs, who left when Adam did."

Adam stirred on the bench beside Lucy. "Adam hide Lucy in the bulrushes," he said.

"A clearing off the Aylesbury road," said Harry. "I found a child's mitten there. The mate to one your father kept."

"Geoffrey ran away," said Adam.

Harry shook his head. "Adam, you were frightened. You thought Geoffrey ran away. But he went to the road to show the French the way." Harry turned to the big man. "I take it that Radcliffe got his start with the money paid to him for betraying the countess."

The big man nodded. "He never stopped working for England's enemies, but he wanted out when the Russian spy Malikov was arrested." The big man turned to another stranger, a tall, dark-haired young gentleman, standing apart from the rest, leaning against the mantel with an amused look on his long, lean face. He had held Hannah when she fled.

"Is that when he came to you?" the big man asked.

The tall stranger pushed off the mantel. "I went to him. We had an encounter over Radcliffe's practice of disposing of his dead animals on my land. I threatened to expose him and offered to buy up all his cattle. He had another idea. He would pay me to play highwayman and 'steal' his horses." The stranger shrugged.

The russet-haired big man grinned. "Let's talk," he said.

A stir at the door signaled the arrival of the constables and a magistrate. Harry's dark-haired friend came to tell them each would be summoned to give witness.

*For the woman of property, the question of when to accept
a gentleman's proposal may be vexed. Knowing, from her own
experience, the cares and satisfactions of managing her affairs
allows her to meet her suitors on an equal footing. She is of all
women free to choose the husband of her heart without regard
to the acquisition of a comfortable establishment for her future
life. Furthermore, she does not expect a man of sense himself to
deny the advantages of a pretty piece of property or a handsome
income with which to supply the needs of a household. She
does not wish to marry a fool or a spendthrift. Nevertheless,
she must accept no proposal until she is fully convinced that
a gentleman's passion for her person wholly outweighs his
interest in her purse.*

—*The Husband Hunter's Guide to London*

Chapter 23

By nine the spies had returned to the club. It was the first time they'd
returned since the night of Jane Fawkener's kidnapping. They lit fires and
candles in the vast coffee room, and now had sandwiches and coffee to
sustain them. After serving them with Miranda's help, Wilde had slipped
away to sit with the girl and her father above Kirby's shop. Goldsworthy
had deigned to join them.

"Well, lads," Goldsworthy said, "we've had a triumph today."

"Will Chartwell think so?" Hazelwood asked. Chartwell in the Foreign
Office ultimately controlled the purse strings for all of them.

Goldsworthy nodded. With his size he took up an entire sofa. "It's a
promising step in getting our operation going again. And with..."

"With?" Blackstone prompted.

Goldsworthy waved one of his great hands in the air. "Never mind.
You lot have done well. You've done your duty. It's time to put down your
weapons. A year and a day. That's the term of service England asked of
you, and you gave it in full measure. A man should do no more."

He frowned, and for a moment looked weary. "Any longer and a man
changes, loses himself," he said. He heaved himself up from his couch.

"Mountjoy," he said to Harry. "You'll be off tomorrow?"

"I will," Harry agreed. In the morning he would begin his new life.
He had a brother to bury and an estate to reclaim from ruin. In time, he

supposed, duty and work would fade his memories of a golden girl with laughter in her eyes.

The blacksmith Will Wittering had stood in the crowd in the inn common room, watching Harry's departure. If Wittering had an ounce of patience in his nature, he would bide his time and wait for the rhythms of the Tooth and Nail to draw Lucy back into her old life. Compared to Brook Street the inn might look shabby, but compared to Mountjoy, it was a palace.

* * * *

The day after Mountjoy again walked out of her life was a beef day, wet and windy outside and smelling of Mrs. Vell's roast inside. The inn door banged frequently as neighbors and strangers alike came to view the broken Waterloo case and hear one of the bench sitters tell the tale of Geoffrey Radcliffe's dramatic end. Little groups gathered in the entry looking down at the common room, with John Simkins or Will Wittering pointing to the spot where the rich man had died.

She sat with Adam on the bench. She gave him silver to polish, but his hands fell idle every few minutes as if he'd forgotten his work. He cocked his head to listen to the talk whenever Harry Clare's name was mentioned. When Adam began to doze, she led him back to his bed. He lay down willingly, and she set Hannah to watch over him. The girl had not fully recovered from the fright of the day before, and Lucy gave her mending to keep her busy.

She retreated to her own room to write some necessary letters to her friends and to her uncle, explaining her discovery of her mother's name and background, and telling them firmly and lovingly that her new knowledge did not alter the fixed attachments of her heart. In her letter to her uncle she mentioned that she had in her possession a painting of her mother, and should he wish to visit the inn, he would be most welcome to see it.

She looked at the laughing lady on her wall, her mother, with new eyes now. She was, after all, a spy, and Lucy was a spy's daughter. You and I, she told the lady in the picture, must become better acquainted.

She folded her letters and sealed them. She understood Harry Clare, Mountjoy, better now. He had not abandoned the idea of marrying her because he thought an innkeeper's daughter beneath him, but rather because he thought the proprietress of a thriving inn could look higher in life than a spy and the ruined son of a disreputable earl.

The second day of her life apart from Harry Clare she woke to a regular snowstorm with whirling flakes. It was a pork day.

On the third day another heavy fall of snow in the night had silenced the birds. Lamb again. And a second proposal from Will Wittering.

*In the end the husband hunter must choose one gentleman.
She must put to rest all other possibilities for her happiness.
In that moment of declaring her acceptance of a gentleman's
proposal, she seems to be making a momentous choice that
fixes her identity as the wife of a particular man. It appears
that she is no longer to be Miss Potential, but Lady Defined.
Yet the truth of her choosing is really quite different. Dozens of
handsome, witty, charming men will remain in London. She will
be as lovely and captivating herself with a ring on her finger as
she was before her wedding day. The moment she chooses her
husband is but the first time she chooses him. Far from ending
the necessity of choosing, that day commits her to a path on
which she must choose him again and again all the days of their
life together.*

—*The Husband Hunter's Guide to London*

Chapter 24

Harry opened the inn door at that quiet hour before the afternoon stage arrived. Cold air swirled behind him, warmth met him. He stood in the shadows of the entrance landing, breathing Mrs. Vell's roast, snow on his hat and greatcoat. He glanced at the Waterloo case. The broken glass had been replaced, and his old sword returned to its place. The last battle had been won.

Across the room Adam sat on his bench, his head tilted toward the open door, alert as a sentry. Beside the old man Lucy reached a hand to recall him to his task. Harry took a moment to watch her unobserved. Then he shook the snow from his hat and coat and hung them on the familiar hook. It was time to claim his love.

First he had to pass through the common room and the tap. One of the few bench sitters spotted him at the foot of the stairs and gave a shout.

Lucy lifted her head from the needlework in her lap. He met her gaze, and the cold of the journey left him.

The bench sitters rose to surround him and shake his hand or clap him on the back. He let them buy him a drink, surprised at how at ease he felt in their company. He was home now.

"Do you make a long stay this time, Captain?"

He nodded. He did not correct them about his title. "Excuse me, gentlemen," he said. He put his ale cup on the bar and crossed to where Lucy and Adam sat.

"Hello, Adam, it's Harry," he said.

"You like your ale very dark, Captain," Adam replied.

"I do," Harry agreed. He let himself look at his love, her gray eyes full of mirth, her face a rare day of English sunshine, golden dappled beauty. He wanted to hear her laugh.

"So, you've come," she said.

"You probably knew I would before I knew it myself."

She nodded. "Mr. Goldsworthy paid us a visit."

"It took three days for his express to reach me," Harry explained.

"The express mattered a great deal, I suppose," she said.

"It did to me. When a man courts a woman of property, he wishes to be beforehand in the world."

"And are you—"

"I bought back Richard's mortgages. Mountjoy belongs to the Clares again." He realized a heartbeat too late what she was asking.

"—courting a woman of property?" she finished with a smile.

Adam came to Harry's rescue. "Captain, you happy at the inn."

"I am," Harry said. He took Adam's hand and received one of Adam's vigorous, two-pump handshakes.

"Queenie ran away," Adam announced.

"I'm sorry," Harry replied. He sat on the bench next to his old friend and stretched out his legs.

"Still have Lucy," the old man continued. "Lucy safe."

"Thank you for keeping Lucy safe, Adam."

"You stay here, Captain?"

Harry looked at Lucy. "If a certain room is available, I'd like to stay the night," he said. It seemed to him a long time, possibly as long as the interval between two heartbeats, before she answered.

"I think we have just the room for you, Lord Mountjoy."

* * * *

There was the usual inn business to be got through, stage passengers to feed, the tap to close, lingering guests to send off to bed, and Adam to care for, before it was time for Lucy to follow her love upstairs. She found him sitting by the fire in the inn's best room, the one her father had chosen for him weeks earlier. He had made himself comfortable in his shirt and trousers, his stocking feet stretched out, a glass of wine in one hand. She could not imagine he felt her sense of raging impatience.

Then their gazes met and held.

"I couldn't be sure you would come." He had not moved, but she sensed some internal shift in him.

"How could I not after you invited Radcliffe to shoot you rather than me?"

"I couldn't bear it if he shot you."

"Ah," she said. "I felt the same way about his shooting you. The point was to be together."

"And so you're here."

She nodded.

"I have to kiss you," he said, and he moved, easily and swiftly, so that she hardly noticed how he managed the wine and the chair and crossing the room.

"I rather hoped you would."

And he did, taking her in his arms and crushing her to him, matching her in impatience to kiss and touch. He deepened the kiss and lifted her from her feet so that her body pressed down on his. The kiss went on while the fire cracked and hissed until he groaned in his throat and set her down, their breath rasping.

They paused and laughed, and he glanced at the bed. She read his intention and took his hand, willing to be led. He took a shuddering breath.

"Wait," he said. He retrieved a small velvet box from the jacket hanging over his chair. He knelt on the rug before her and lifted up the open box. A band of gold and rubies sparkled in the velvet folds. "Will you marry me and be my lady?"

He had forgotten an important line. She would remind him later, but she nodded her *yes*, extending her hand, allowing him to slide his ring onto her finger, pulling him up from his knees.

He glanced again at the bed, drawing a deep steadying breath, a sign, she knew, that he was going to be far too honorable for her feelings at the moment.

"Can we be married tomorrow, do you think? In London? Don't they have ways, special licenses and such?"

A particularly broad grin erased all that was harsh in his face. "They do. We can," he said, getting her drift, because he was not slow, her love.

She laughed then, and he pulled her to the bed and brought them both down upon it.

Harry rolled her under him, sensing her impatience, kissing and touching, pulling up her skirts, pushing her legs apart and fitting himself into the sweet hollow of her body where he could press and rock against her. He slid his hands over thin cotton stockings, finding the silken skin above her garters. She moaned and opened wider to his hand, and he shifted to cup her woman's place through her damp drawers, using his thumb to find the nub of her pleasure.

She moaned at the touch, her arms going slack around him, lying back, looking up at him, panting and breathless, wonder in her gray eyes.

He grinned at her. "You like that."

"I do," she said.

"There's more," he said, "but let's get rid of some of these clothes."

He rocked back on his knees and pulled her up. She turned so he could undo the fastenings along her back. He pushed her gown down over her shoulders and pulled the pins from her hair, letting it spill down, enjoying the springy waves of it. He buried his face briefly in that hair before he turned her again to make short work of her front-fastening stays.

He tossed the practical corset aside and pulled her chemise over her head and gave his full attention to her breasts, cupping them and rubbing his thumbs across the tight buds, making her arch up to his touch.

Lucy had not imagined her breasts capable of such sensation. From the tips he touched so gently, first with his thumbs and then with his mouth, streaks of pleasure shot to her woman's place, making it ache and weep for him. She squirmed impatiently in the crumpled folds of her skirts.

"Now you," she said to him.

He grinned again and slipped off the bed, drawing her after him, so that he stood at the edge of the bed in the little cove of her legs. She helped him pull the shirt up over his ribs and chest, and he tossed it aside. His hands went to the fall of his trousers, and she reached to help him.

Harry shed wool and linen in a single swift move and stood before her. He did not have to tell her to look. She gave him a very frank appraisal, even his cockstand. There was no fear or distaste in her look, only curiosity and, he thought, impatience to touch. He took her hand, putting it to his swollen flesh, showing her the rhythm they would share.

He pushed her back on the bed and tugged away the last of her clothes.

They were skin to skin at last. He put the tip of his aching flesh to hers, sliding against her slick folds, still holding back, waiting for her to arch and open under him.

Lucy needed something more. She arched up against him, and with a quick flex of his hips he accomplished their joining. It surprised her, the unexpected pinch of it, and at same time, the unexpected rightness of the way her body held his so perfectly. She was an innkeeper and she knew a thing or two about welcoming a guest and making him at home, so she waited for the burn to pass and smiled up into his face taut with pleasure.

"I love you," she said.

He lowered himself to his elbows and kissed her, his mouth touching hers as light as air. "I love you," he replied.

She closed her eyes at the words she'd been waiting for and lifted her hips to meet his, and together they began to move to a shared beat. She felt herself stroking like a swimmer for a distant shore, swells pushing her onward, until a great surge lifted her.

He whispered, "Now," and as he convulsed, she shuddered with a pleasure so intense it robbed her breath. The sweet lingering note of it vibrated in her as she descended from the peak. She felt him slide from her and take her into his arms, holding her like the dearest thing he had.

* * * *

Later as they lay warm, damp, and naked in each other's arms, Lucy stirred against his chest, her right hand tracing patterns on his ribs that he found promising. She meant to test him.

"You came looking for Adam."

"I did. Goldsworthy had an informant who said there was an important witness we had to find, a blind man."

"There must be other blind men in London."

"Yes, but none who were being pursued by hired bully boys. When I found Adam, your father and I had a frank talk about the danger."

"So my father knew you were a spy?"

"He did. We made an arrangement." He pushed himself up against the pillows and pulled her up with him, her head against his chest. He did not mean to let go of her until they got over this rough patch of ground.

"For you to stay at the inn."

"To keep an eye out for whoever meant Adam harm."

"In exchange for?"

"Well, your father conceived of the idea of the Waterloo case, and he warned me that you were meant to be a lady, not a man's fancy piece."

"You didn't tell him that what you wanted was Adam's story, his testimony really."

"No."

Harry tried to keep his heartbeat steady. Her hand with the ruby ring now made circles around his left nipple. "Do you want to change your

mind about marrying me?" It was only fair to ask, now that she knew
more of the truth.

Again he waited. She flattened her palm over his heart.

"No," she said. "I think it's entirely fitting for a spy's daughter to marry
a spy." And she lifted her head from his chest and looked at him with those
laughing eyes. Her hair fell in golden curls around her face. "So, my lord
spy, what do you mean to do next?"

He laughed and shifted her above him, taking in the pale rosy tips of
her breasts, and the narrowness of her waist in his hands. "Now," he said,
"I mean to lie back and think of England." And he pulled her down and
kissed her.

* * * *

Lucy said goodbye to her inn on a beef day. While Mountjoy saw to
their cases and helped Adam to dress, she went round the inn in the early
light, opening shutters and doors, saying farewell to each thing she touched.

As she opened the kitchen door, a loud hoarse mewing greeted her. On
the step, crouched over the body of a large gray rat, was a creature she
hardly recognized, a scrawny cat whose dirt-caked fur stuck out in matted
clumps. Its left ear was torn, and a long scratch aslant its face made the
eye weepy.

Lucy knelt, reaching out a hand, and the creature arched into her touch,
trembling. "Oh Queenie, you brought me a gift. Come inside."

They had a brief cat and mistress debate about the proper disposal of
the dead rat, but in the end, coaxed by a pot of cream, Queenie left the rat
on the steps. She crouched over the bowl of cream, lapping hungrily until
Mrs. Vell arrived and shrieked to see such a filthy animal in her kitchen.

Lucy coaxed Queenie with more cream to the laundry for a bath.

Harry, looking in from the laundry door, found her up to her elbows in
dirty water and outraged cat. "Ah," he said, "here's where you've got to.
Adam and I wondered."

Lucy lifted Queenie, her legs extended, claws spread, onto the washboard
and poured a pitcher of clear water over her. Queenie shook wildly. "Poor
dear, she's been mauled terribly. What do you think happened to her?"

"Radcliffe had someone take her," Harry said. "He saw, as Nate did,
that Adam used her as his sentry, warning him of danger. Whoever took
her dumped her, in the river, I suspect."

"Can you hold that towel for me?" Lucy asked.

Harry stepped up next to Lucy and picked up the old towel she had lying there.

She watched his eyes shift from the towel to the bath to the wet front of her gown. "You," she said, "are not thinking of Queenie."

He swallowed. "You know, if you need a bath, I am more than willing to hold your towel."

"Are you?" She laughed and watched his face change again, promising that last night had been only the start of their lovemaking. She held up the dripping, indignant cat and let her love wrap the creature in the towel.

* * * *

In the end, Lucy managed to change her gown without her husband-to-be's assistance, though she promised he could be her bath attendant as soon as they were married. Their carriage was at the door, and the inn people lined up to send them off. Adam sat on his bench with Hannah at his side. Queenie, her fur dried to an orange-and-white fluff, lay in his lap, her face pressed against his thigh, asleep with his big hands around her. Lucy kissed the old man's gaunt cheek. He was at peace at last. They all were, the soldiers home from their wars.

Not least of the pleasures of the happy ending of the husband hunter's hunt is the talk that now engages husband and wife in recounting the progress of their love. Who first began to love? What signs did each observe or fail to observe in the other? What mistakes were made and what obstacles had to be overcome? What irresistible longings could only be answered in a lasting union of minds and hearts? Such is the power of the story of a prosperous love that the lovers delight in retelling it though their heads be gray and their joined hands wrinkled.

—*The Husband Hunter's Guide to London*

Epilogue

Nate Wilde watched Miranda pour perfect rich coffee from the frothing pot into the tiny cups they used at the club. While his shoulder healed, he was teaching her how to make coffee the way the old soldier had taught him when he first left Bread Street.

With her brains and her clever seamstress's hands, she caught on quickly. She poured the last of the coffee into a closed pot for keeping and put the pot on the silver tray they would carry up to the club coffee room. The club was open again, and Goldsworthy wanted his new recruit to receive the club's best. Ajax Lynley.

Goldsworthy had given Miranda a lot of credit for bringing Nate through their adventure. She had confessed to him what she'd told Nate about the note she had failed to give Jane Fawkener. Goldsworthy had looked quite grim at that, but he had told her she was a brave girl, and that she'd do.

Nate kissed her. It was agreed between them now that he could kiss her whenever and wherever their circumstances permitted until that day she came of age. Then they would marry, and Nate could love her in all the ways he had not yet let himself think about loving her. And with the club open there was a chance that even a fellow like him, born on Bread Street, could become a Sir someday and call his wife Lady Wilde.

Read on for a preview of Kate Moore's next Husband Hunter's Guide romance, available in spring 2019.

Of all the gentlemen in London, the attractive rogue poses the greatest danger to the husband hunter's happiness.

—*The Husband Hunter's Guide to London*

Chapter 1

Lady Emily Radstock accepted a greeting from her sister's butler Gittings and handed him her coat, gloves, and bonnet. She dispensed with Gittings's attempt to precede her up to the drawing room. He mumbled something as she bounded past him, her package under her arm. She assured him she did not need to be announced. Gittings was sixty if he was a day, and Lady Emily was in a hurry.

As she threw open the drawing room door, her younger sister, Rosalind, sitting at her needlework, her stocking feet up on a blue velvet ottoman, looked up with a start.

"Where is she?" Emily demanded. The door closed behind her.

"Hello, Em. Where is who?" Rosalind held up a delicate white gown no bigger than a tea towel.

"Mother," said Emily. She strode across the room to stand before her sister, looking down. Rosalind, six years younger than Emily and rosy and round with her first pregnancy, made a strikingly domestic appearance.

"Oh, Mother's gone to Grandmama's."

Emily sank onto the sofa opposite her sister's chair. "Of all the cowardly dodges. She knows she's safe from me there."

"What's she done?" Rosalind asked, lowering the white garment to her lap.

"This!" said Emily, tossing the package she carried onto the small gateleg table next to Rosalind. The package made a satisfying slap against the polished wood.

Rosalind regarded it warily. "She's offended you with a brown paper package tied up in string."

"No. Yes. Come to think of it, I am offended by the brown paper and the string, her idea of being discreet before the servants."

"Em, you must enlighten me. I'm growing more confused by the minute."

"Sorry, Roz. Were you napping?" Emily realized that half the drapery over the tall windows had been drawn to shadow the far end of the room, where Rosalind had stationed a spectacular camel back sofa in a deep green and peony-patterned damask their mother had given her. The sofa had been turned to face away from the blues and golds of the room's main seating arrangement.

"No, I drew the drapery because—"

"How are you?" Emily asked.

"Quite well really. A great many of the discomforts have passed and the terrible fatigue. That's why Mother thought she could go to Grandmama, who really does need her more than I do at the moment. And I have Philip," she said brightly.

"Is Phil much help?" Emily asked. "I didn't know husbands were."

"He is." Rosalind smiled in what Emily thought was a rather dreamy way for a married woman about to bear a child. "But you came to tell me what's upset you."

"Husbands. Or rather my lack of one and what Mother chose to do about it. As if it were her problem. Open the package, Roz, you'll see."

"You know what's inside, Em?"

"I do. Open it."

Rosalind put aside her needlework and took up the little package, untying the string and pulling off the paper. She glanced at Emily and read the title on a small blue volume. "*The Husband Hunter's Guide to London*?"

"You see," said Emily, "wrapped up as if it were a gift and left for Alice to bring up with my chocolate this morning while Mama has gone off to avoid me."

"It's not a gift?" asked Rosalind, turning the pages of the little blue book, her gaze skimming over them.

"A gift?" Emily bounced a little on the sofa. "It's a notice to vacate. It's a shove out of the nest. It's a lit fuse on a bomb."

Rosalind looked up. "Surely, Mama means nothing of the kind."

"Doesn't she? It's my birthday in three weeks. I'll be twenty-nine. She considers me past hope. Now she's given me a book for a schoolroom chit."

"Do you think so? You don't really want to continue at home, do you? You want an establishment of your own."

"Of course I do. But it won't be my establishment, will it? It will belong to some man, and it will be my job to run it for him."

Rosalind shook her head. "I don't think marriage...should be seen in exactly that light."

Emily stared at the rather magnificent painting of a chestnut stallion over the marble hearth. "You know, Roz, I should marry the first imbecile I meet, however brainless or idle he is."

"Darling, I don't think you should do anything so desperate."

The door to the sitting room opened, and a young man of fair ruddy good looks entered and stopped with a furrowed brow when he spotted Emily. "Hello, Em," he said. "I thought..." He looked around the room as if it were a puzzle to be solved.

"Phil, dear?" Rosalind gave him one of her dreamy smiles.

He crossed the room and gave his wife a quick kiss on the cheek. "Roz," he said, "I'm looking for Lynley. I thought Gittings said he showed him up to you, but I find Em instead."

"Oh dear," said Roz. "I forgot all about Lynley."

"Where is he then?" Phil asked.

"Right here, old man." A tall, dark-haired giant with a lean face, elegantly dressed limbs, and an indolent manner unfolded himself from behind the camel back sofa. He fixed his gaze on Emily.

"You should have made yourself known, sir." Emily waited for her hair to catch on fire from the heat of the blush in her cheeks.

The giant moved her way with easy grace. "I think you've proposed to me," he said. "And I accept."

Emily had been trained all her life not to stare, but nothing could stop her from gaping up into the handsome, amused face staring down at her.

"Shall I put the announcement in the papers?" The giant took her hand, gave it a quick kiss, and turned to her brother-in-law. "At your service, Phil."

With a bow and a look of supreme satisfaction, he took his leave.

About the Author

Kate Moore is a former English teacher and three-time RITA finalist, and Golden Heart and Book Buyers Best award winner. She writes Austen-inspired fiction set in nineteenth-century England or contemporary California. Her heroes are men of courage, competence, and unmistakable virility, with determination so strong it keeps their sensuality in check until they meet the right woman. Her heroines take on the world with practical good sense and kindness to bring those heroes into a circle of love and family. Sometimes there's even a dog. Kate lives north of San Francisco with her surfer husband, their yellow Lab, a Pack 'n Play for visiting grandbabies, and miles of crowded bookshelves. Kate's family and friends offer endless support and humor. Her children are her best works, and her husband is her favorite hero. Visit Kate at Facebook.com/KateMooreAuthor or contact her at kate@katemoore.com.

Printed in the United States
by Baker & Taylor Publisher Services